I0691398

Marshmallow Cream
– and Hard Big Pieces of Chocolate

First Edition

Published by The Nazca Plains Corporation
Las Vegas, Nevada
2009

ISBN: 978-1-935509-42-4

Published by

The Nazca Plains Corporation ®
4640 Paradise Rd, Suite 141
Las Vegas NV 89109-8000

PUBLISHER'S NOTE
Marshmallow Cream – and Hard Big Pieces of Chocolate is a work of fiction created wholly by *Wade Wright's* imagination. All characters are fictional and any resemblance to any persons living or deceased is purely by accident. No portion of this book reflects any real person or events.

Male Cover Photo, C Quenum
Marshmallow and Chocolate, Robert Gubbins
Art Director, Blake Stephens

Dedication

To every living individual that knows the experiences of knowing, and hopefully loving, another individual that is somewhat different than they are, as in the case of, one black man and one white man, or one married man, and one single man!

Marshmallow Cream
– and Hard Big Pieces of Chocolate

First Edition

Wade Wright

Contents

Contents continued...

Two Hunky Neighbors

Chapter One: In The Pool

"Hey, Jim, turn around!" Bob yelled at his friend and neighbor as Jim pulled himself up and out of the backyard pool at Bob's house.

Jim was in the process of wiping himself off with one of the towels stacked on the table beside the pool. "Hey Jim!" Bob continued, "Hey guy, turn around!"

Using the towel to cover his crotch area, but attempting to make it appear as if he was continuing to wipe himself dry, he finally did turn and look at Bob, who was still in the pool, and who was looking at Jim, but also toward the house and the door to make sure that neither of the wives were coming back out to the pool area. He told Jim, "Drop the towel!"

With a big question in his voice, Jim asked Bob, "What? Why?"

Moving up close to the edge of the pool, Bob then very quietly stated, "Because I want to see your crotch!"

"What!? What did you say?" Jim asked in earnest.

"Move your towel!" Bob rather insisted.

"Why, why? Why do you want me to do that?" Jim again asked.

Very quietly Bob responded, as he once again turned and looked toward the house to make sure it was still just the two men at the pool, "Because Jim,

I know you are sporting a woody, and I want to see it. Come on, get back in the pool!"

Quickly, Jim rather threw the towel toward the table and immediately jumped back into the pool. He had a very quizzed look on his face, but nonetheless, he jumped back into the water.

Jim and Bob were neighbors, living in houses directly across the street from each other, and since they were close to the same ages, Bob being 29 and Jim being 30, they had become very good friends, since Jim and Suzzie had moved in about a year and a half earlier. Bob and Judy did enjoy their company, and Bob had suggested the four of them getting together and having pool parties quite often, and as often as possible. Since neither couple had any children, the socializing was easy and convenient. Much more so than with couples that had children that needed to be included or worried about.

Bob knew he liked having Jim in the pool, so that the two of them could just do some good old goofing around, as if they were still little kids.

Bob moved over toward Jim, once Jim re-entered into the water and said, "Jim, I've been pretty damn sure the last three or four times that we've been in the pool together that you are getting a stiffy when we touch each other, and that's why I put those towels on that table, instead of over by the door. I wanted to see if you'd get a towel and cover yourself before you turned around, and yip, you did! Jim, haven't you kind of noticed that the last couple of times we've swum together that I've been a little more active in kind of wrestling with you in the water? Jim, every time I get a chance, I attempt to rub up against your rod, and every time, it's hard!"

With that statement made, this time Bob was very straight forward and actually reached out, and under the water he cupped his hand on Jim's crotch. Jim rather jerked in the surprise of being touched, and especially by his friend and neighbor Bob, but he did not pull away.

Bob looked into Jim's eyes and slightly smiled. Jim continued to silently stand there, but much more due to shock than for any other reason. He did not move. He did not return the grope.

Bob turned so that he was facing the house door and quietly told Jim, "Jim, I've been wanting to feel this thing since the first time you came over here swimming. When you and Suzzie moved in, the very first time you guys came over for a swim, I could swear you got hard when we were playing around and goofing off with that pool ball. My arm accidentally rubbed against your crotch, and I was sure then you had a boner. You did, didn't you?"

Kind in a state of shock, Jim answered, "Yeah, I think I did. Yeah, I probably did, but I didn't know you knew it! It was all by accident!"

"Yeah I know Jim, they've all been by accident, haven't they? Jim, I have a boner every time we are in the pool together. I've watched you get out of the pool every time you've been in here with me, and you always hide behind something till you get rid of your stiffer, so that's why I put the towels over there so you'd have to turn around or let it be obvious you were hiding something. Right? Hey Jim, I know you are shocked, but feel my crotch. You're not the only one in here that's got a boner. Mine's stiff too! I like feeling you, and I know you like feeling me too, don't you?"

Bob took hold of Jim's right hand and directed it toward his own crotch. Jim very slowly reached forward and slightly touched Bob's crotch.

Very quietly and rather embarrassingly, Jim managed a slight, "Yeah," but then continued, "Bob, I've never been in a situation like this before. Bob, you are getting me all confused here. Bob, our wives are in the house. Don't do anything that can get us in trouble, OK?"

"Oh hell no Jim! I won't! But I've finally let you know that I want to do something, so now it's too late to act like nothing ever happened!"

"Yeah, well yeah — I guess you're right!" Jim replied.

Just as Jim was responding, Suzzie and Judy came out of the house and Suzzie, asked, "Hey are you guys going to get out of the pool and get ready to go?"

Slightly moving away from each other a little, and only slightly so the wives would not think anything funny about the men standing so close to each other, Jim then said, "Hey gals! Bob and I have been talking, and we really are not very excited about going to that show! It's just not our bag! It's all about love, dating, marriage and all that stuff, and hey, there's a baseball game on the TV tonight, and we were kind of wondering if maybe we could just stay here and watch the game, and let you two wonderful — beautiful — talented, and — successful women have a ladies night out, all by yourselves? Is that possible?"

Looking at Judy, Suzzie then replied, "Well, after all of those complements, how can we turn those guys down? How about we just tell them that dinner will now be included in our night out, and it will be on their credit cards? What do you say?"

"Judy laughed, and replied, "Hell yes! What a deal! I've been wanting to go to that new fancy Italian restaurant down on Stanley Drive, and this just might be the best time to do it!" Then looking at the husbands, Judy added, "Hell yes men! Hell yes! We'll let you watch your ole baseball game. Miss Suzzie and I take you up on your offer! After you see how much we can add to

3

your credit cards, for just one dinner, I'm sure you might have different ideas the next time though! Right, Suzzie?"

"Right! Damn right Judy! And I sure am not going to that place looking like this! I need to go change into something nice and fancy! We are really going to have one hell of a women's night out! Come on Judy, let them swim and do their thing watching their ole TV baseball! We have things to do!" Then looking at Jim, Suzzie asked, "Hey, what are you two going to do for dinner? What are you going to eat?"

As Jim looked at Bob, he simply asked, "Pizza? Yeah, yeah — we'll order some pizza to have with our game! Hey, don't worry bout us, we will survive. We'll do OK! You gals go do your ladies night out thing. We'll take care of each other and act like bachelors again for a night!"

With that statement, the two wives turned and returned to the house.

"Oh shit man! Jim that was one fast thinking! Thanks man! Sounds like it is going to cost us some cash, I've heard that restaurant is damn expensive, but hey, let them do their thing and then we can do our thing! Besides, the cost of those dinners can't be more than if we had bought actual tickets to the game, so maybe we are still ahead."

"Yeah, and Bob, as soon as they hit the road, then we'll be able to do some skinny dipping here. I've got to admit, I've wanted to do that since the first time you and Judy invited us over for a swim, but I always kind of figured the women just might not go for that."

"Yeah—the women, and probably me too, since I know damn well running around the pool, bare assed naked and everything hanging out, I'd never been able to explain why my dick was harder out here than it is in the bedroom."

After about 20 minutes of just "hanging out" in the pool, sipping some beers and eating some chips, the men were then interrupted by Judy as she poked her head out of the door and yelled, "Hey guys! I'm all dolled up and ready for our gals night out, so I'm headed over to Suzzie's and then we are "out on the town!" Jim, we're using your car since the sports car is much more to our liking for a night like tonight, than that four-door thing of ours, so anyway, we'll be back later. Oh hey, the show starts at 7, it's about an hour and a half long, so I'm told, and then of course we girls will need to go have a night cap someplace nice and fancy before we get home so we'll probably be back about 10 or ten thirty. OK?"

Bob had moved over to her side of the pool as she was talking and after she finished, Bob motioned for her to bend down so that he could give her a kiss, and he then told her to have fun, but be safe. "We'll see you ladies later! Have fun!" Bob added.

"Have fun!" Jim added with a yell from the far side of the pool.

"Oh I'm sure we will!" Judy hollered back. "You TV jocks have fun too!"

As Jim waved a good-bye, he silently said, "Oh we will honey, we will!"

Waiting a few minutes to make sure they were actually by themselves, Jim did get out of the pool and peaked through the yard gate to see if he could see his own driveway from that spot. "Hey Bob, they are just now driving out! They are on their way! It's just you and me now man!"

As Jim made that statement, he then turned toward the pool, slid his thumbs under the waistband of his beach trunks, and pulled them down and then stepped out of them. Rock hard dick and all, Jim was now completely displaying his athletic 5'11" frame, his 44 inch chest, his 34 inch waist, his 17" calves and of course his 15-15 1/2 inch biceps.

As he threw his shorts to a chair, he flipped his dick once in a playful manner and jumped into the pool.

Seeing that his swimming partner was now a nude swimmer, Bob immediately removed his Speedos and threw them up on the pool deck.

"OK man!" Jim stated firmly. "I paraded my bare assed self across the deck, letting you see all of me, now get out of the pool and let me see how you are hung!"

Grinning broadly and rather laughing, Bob did pull himself up and onto the pool edge so that he too would be showing everything as Jim had just done. As he pushed up onto the deck, and then lifted one leg up to get his foot onto the deck, he realized that he was making a formal presentation of his bare ass and it's hairy hole to his neighbor friend and his now male, nude, swim mate. He truly liked the idea that he and Jim were now completely naked in front of each other and he was proud that he had already had the opportunity to show Jim his bare ass, with his legs rather spread, without making a major issue out of it. He was hoping that his bag was hanging down nicely, and was completely visible under his ass, since he knew his stick was standing up by his stomach and definitely was not visible from behind. He was hoping that Jim was noticing his hairy ass and his full bag, and was liking what he was seeing.

Bob too was another very hot specimen of a hunk, standing right at 5'10", 190 pounds, a solid firm chest of about 42" and a 32" waist, and legs and arms that were just a little stockier than Jim's. Firm and of course standing straight out and up, his dick was 7 1/2 inches long and a thick 5-inch circumference when measured around it when hard, as it definitely was now. It was finally being presented to his friend, as he had been wanting to do for a long time now, and it was at its full attention. The slight trail of fuzz hair, positioned just above his navel and extending up toward his square chin, completed the manly picture of "all hunk!"

"Oh my God!" Jim exclaimed! "Shit man, no fucking wonder I get hard when we are in the pool together! Bob how in the hell do you manage to hide that thing when all you have on are Speedos? Damn man! I knew you showed what looked like a lot in those Speedos, but my God man, how in the hell do you put that much in there? Shit man! I had no idea you were that fucking well hung! You're a fucking horse, man!"

Feeling very proud of himself, but yet very embarrassed about Jim's very strong and positive comments, Bob jumped back into the pool as if to hide his pole. Immediately, Jim got up close to Bob and grabbed hold of Bob's cock.

"Oh shit man, I have never taken another man's cock in my hand before, but I've got to feel this one! You're making it too damn easy for me to do stuff that I'd never think about doing — but the way you are doing stuff today, I guess it's OK if I do this, right? Damn man! Shit! God Bob, I've never seen a cock this fucking big before!"

As Jim reached out and grabbed a grip onto Bob's enormous stiff rod, Bob also reached forward and put Jim's stiff meat into his hand and squeezed it.

"Jim my buddy, this one don't feel so damn small either, though! Hey, I've got to admit that it's been a hell of a long time since I've had some other guy's dick in my hand, but this one does not feel little at all. Not at all!"

"Been a long time since you had some other guy's dick in your hand!? Bob, have you played around with guys before?"

"Well, no not really! Once in the locker room in high school we did have a gay guy that everybody knew was gay and once a guy made me a bet that I would not grab that guy's dick, and he'd give me five bucks if I did. Well, since I really needed the five bucks, I agreed to do it. They got the guy, his name was Skip, and they told him what was up and of course he was all for it. He was already stripped so he didn't need to take his pants down or anything, all he needed to do was walk up to me, and stand there. About five guys were all standing there watching which made me nervous, but after looking at it, and of course watching it get bigger and bigger as we looked at it, I finally reached out and put my hand on it. I grabbed hold of it so the guy paying the money did not claim that I had not taken hold of it enough. While I had my hand on it, one of the guys in the group told me to jerk on it, and if I'd jerk on it for at least a full minute, he'd give me another five bucks. Hey man, ten bucks right then was big money so I did. Then another guy said that if I could get Skip to shoot off, he'd give me another five bucks, so of course I figured, why not? I was nervous as hell, but Skip loved it! He wanted anybody to play with him, whenever he could get them to do it, so to him it was a big payoff to have that many guys watch him shoot off! So I guess it was a payday for Skip and me both. I made fifteen bucks and Skip got to shoot off in front of about six guys all at the same time."

"So Bob, is that all of the things you've done, or are there more? Shit man — got to admit hearing about that session in the locker room playing with that guy, has got me all turned on. I never got to do anything like that, except read some stuff in some dirty mags, but hearing it from a guy that has actually done it, is so hot! Shit man I think I'm about to shoot just from hearing that! Bob, have you done any other stuff? If you have tell me about it! I've never had any conversation like this before and this is really turning me on! Shit man! This is hot stuff! This is hot shit!"

"You sure this is really hot stuff to you and if I do admit that I've done some other stuff, you won't think bad of me? I really did not intent to talk about what I've done, I was just kind of hoping to maybe play with you some."

"Oh shit Bob! You keep telling me about some stuff like what you were just telling me and I know damn well we will be playing with each other, since right now you've got me about to go totally crazy with excitement. God Bob, I've never been around the types of guys that I guess you have. I've never even been close to being able to touch some other guy, let alone jerk him off. Bob I've tried to find the kinds of dirty magazines that had stories in them like this, and I never thought I'd actually get to talk to some guy that has done some of this stuff. What else have you done?"

"Well, I did get fucked in the ass once."

"Oh shit man, when? What happened? Bob tell me what happened and what was that like?"

"Well, it was that Skip guy again. It was after high school though. I was back home for a weekend and true, I was not having much fun. All the guys that I grew up with all had their own stuff to do, and I didn't have anybody to hang out with. I was in the little local coffee shop and Skip came in. Since we of course did know each other, he sat beside me at the counter and we started talking. Anyway, before the conversation was all over, and after we laughed about some of our high school days, and of course that one specific day in the locker room, he leaned over real close to me and whispered that he wanted to fuck my ass. He asked me if I had ever had that done. I of course told him, 'No,' I sure had not had that done, and he said he was sorry about that."

"He was sorry about — what? That you had never had your ass fucked? Is that what you mean?"

"Yeah, that is what I mean! Yeah, said that he was sorry I had never been fucked before, and he made it sound so depressing, that I had never had that done, I finally agreed to go with him and find out what he was talking about. Of course, though, since everybody in town knew he was a gay guy, I made him leave first so that we did not walk out of the coffee shop together. I met him at his place after we both left, but of course we left at separate times. After I left the coffee shop I started wondering if we had been quiet enough in our conversation that the waitress did not hear what we had been talking about. I figured, Oh well—if she did, so be it! I couldn't do anything about it then, anyway!"

As Jim stood there in the pool listening, he was now actively rubbing his cock and jerking on it some as he begged for more details from Bob's prior experiences. He truly did not believe that he was actually having this type of a conversation, and especially with a guy that he really did like and admired, a lot! It was almost beyond his comprehension that he and Bob could even have this type of a open conversation, and talk about this kind of stuff like this, so openly!

"What happened? What did you guys do. He fucked your ass, right?"

"Oh yeah, he did! I got to his place and all the lights were off, and he had about eight candles lit around his place. He had a small apartment, so a few candles went a long way, so to say. Have to admit — I had never been is such a romantic place as his apartment was that night. He opened the door, and I guess he knew I'd be by myself and nobody could see his front door. He was totally naked! He answered his front door completely bare assed! That was the first time that I had ever seen somebody answer their front door completely nude! God — that in itself was a major turn on! Well — of course that was kind of a shock and I will admit now that even then, I found it kind of exciting. Kind of nervy, I guess. I kept thinking, what if it happened to be somebody else at his door instead of me?"

"And so — he did what? You did what?"

"I went in and he flipped his dick at me and said, Well, you've jerked this one off once before, want to do it again? I just kind of looked at it and he knew that I was a little freaked out about being there, so he didn't push it any. He led me into the living room and softly suggested that I sit down and maybe take my shoes off and get comfortable. He went into the kitchen and brought back a couple of beers. I had taken my shoes off by that time, and I tried to act comfortable but I guess my nerves were showing. He sat his beer on the coffee table and then sat down on the floor beside me, so that he could put his arm across my leg. He kind of hugged my leg a little and then reached down between my legs and took hold of my ankle and kind of squeezed it. You gotta remember, I'm sitting there fully clothed, except for my shoes, and he's totally naked, and having a hard-on! Then he asked me if I had done anything with any other guys since that day in the locker room. I told him that no, I had not, but then I did admit that there were a few times at college that I thought maybe I did want to go find some guy, some guy that I didn't even know, and play around with him some, but I never did. That's when he told me, that now he knew why I had agreed to come to his place and get my ass fucked for the first time. He knew that I was hungry for some good gay playing around, and that I was finally admitting it to myself. He assured me that everything was going to be OK, and that before I left, I would be glad I agreed to it. Right then I was not so damn sure! I mean I really wasn't! For a minute or two, I really did think that maybe I just needed to grab my shoes and run. I was nervous! Shit, I was fucking nervous. Here I was, a guy about 21 years old, never played around with a guy other than that one-day in the locker room, and I had agreed to meet him at his place, and I was there for him to fuck my ass! How fucking crazy was I?"

"Oh God Bob, you did have to think you were out of your mind didn't you?"

"Yes, I thought I was more than out of my mind! I knew I was just plain damn crazy! I knew I was fucking crazy."

"Bob, what kept you there? Why didn't you just tell him that you changed your mind?"

Looking squarely at Jim and directly into Jim's eyes, Bob then said, "Jim, I hope like hell I can totally trust you! Man I am telling you stuff that I never even told a therapist once, when I thought I needed help. Jim, I'm laying it all out in front of you. I hope like hell I can trust you! For God's sake man, please don't ever tell Judy or anybody else about this stuff. It would ruin me man! If you ever told anybody, it would totally ruin me!"

"Bob trust me! Trust me! There is no way in hell I would ever tell anybody what you are telling me. Shit man, the idea that you can tell me this stuff is really a complement to me. No way would I ever break your trust in me after you are being so truthful with me! Believe me, trust me!"

"Jim I got arrested for drunken driving one night while I was a freshman at State. I had to spend the night in the city tank. Sometime in the middle of the night, I don't even know what time it was — I played like I was asleep all night, but I wasn't — one guy fucked another guy right there in the middle of that drunk tank! Nobody caught them, well I did, and I really do think a jail guard saw what was happening, but probably figured that if they were both into it, and nobody was having a fit, then let 'em go. Anyway Jim, I laid there and watched that guy get it up in the ass, and I really wanted to be next! Really, I did! Watching that burly guy take his stiff dick out and slide it up in that other guy's butt hole looked exciting to me! I kept acting like I was asleep, but I kept watching them until the big guy got his rocks off in that guy's butt. That night at Skip's apartment, all I could think about was that night in the jug. I was scared shitless but all I could do was remember watching that one guy get it up in the ass from that other guy, and how jealous I was of the guy getting fucked. I just knew that if I did not stay there and let Skip fuck me, I may never get another chance like that!"

"Oh God Bob, you have got me hotter than a pan of boiling water. Shit man, I am going to have to get out of this water or I am going to have cum floating in it. And — that's without even touching it! Bob you have got me turned inside out man!"

"Here Jim, sit up here on the edge of the pool."

"No I can't do that! Thanks Bob, but seriously my dick is so damn hard right now, there is no way I can sit on the edge of the pool and let it fly like a forty foot flag pole. No, I won't cum in the pool, but if I think I'm going to, I promise to get out. OK? God Bob! Tell me! What in the hell happened?"

"Well, I was sitting there and Skip had his arm draped over my right leg and he had a hold on my ankle. He was sitting down on the floor beside me. I was in the chair. Pretty soon he started sliding his hand up and down the inside of my leg. After he did that for a while, I could tell he had his elbow stuck in my crotch and he could tell I was hard. Pretty soon he just kind of turned around and unsnapped my Levi's and pulled them open. I had a pair of briefs on, and of course they were tenting pretty good! Skip told me to stand up, and when I did, he pulled my Levi's and my briefs off. He asked me to pull my T-shirt off. I did! Then he told me to just sit back down. I did! I was shaking like shit, I knew I was, but I think that was a turn on to him. I think he liked having some guy that he knew was scared shitless. And I was! Honestly Jim, all I could think about was that guy in the jail that got it up his ass and how he acted like it felt so good and how he wanted it more, when the big guy pulled out. I remembered hearing him beg the big guy to put it back in again, but the big guy just got up off of his butt and left him laying there in the middle of the floor. Anyway the guy that got fucked then grabbed his pants, pulled them back up and finally just got up and went over to a corner and sat down. That was all I could think about that night while Skip was starting to lick on me. And yeah — he licked! Jim, I had that man's tongue all over me. Hell man, when I take a bath I don't do that thoroughly of a job on my body. He did not miss a spot. I did not know it until that night that some gay guys get real turned on by sucking toes. Shit man, that is something to relish and enjoy! What a fucking feeling to have some guy's tongue up between your toes licking them clean. Doing that must have taken at least a full half an hour. I was sitting there with this ragging hard-on the entire time. I had never been in a situation where I just sat there, and of course completely naked, and watched and felt somebody totally enjoy playing with some part of my body! Jim, that was unbelievable! I kind of felt like my feet were being worshipped! I was sitting there with a ragging hard-on, and he wasn't even touching it!"

"Oh God Bob! I never had any imagination that this day was going to have anything like this in it! Oh shit Bob! I feel like some little kid in a toy store for the very first time. Shit man, tell me what in the hell happened next? What happened?"

"He sucked on my dick!"

"What — oh shit man — he did!? Oh God Bob — keep talking! This is so damn exciting! Oh man, I never thought I'd ever have this kind of a conversation!"

"He had seen it before, while we were in school, and back then I knew he wanted it, but I never let him do it. I kind of think that day in the locker room, there might have been some more stuff planned that just never happened."

"What? Like what? What do you mean?"

"I have thought it through since then, and although I never asked Skip if I was right or not, I really do think that whole thing was kind of a set up to see if I'd let Skip suck me off or not. Yeah, my dick was bigger than all the other guy's, especially when we were a lot younger, and the guys all liked to talk about it and look at it. I really do think it was all set with Skip that if he could get me to fuck his mouth, then those guys would give him some money. I remember back, how some comments were made about how I should let him suck me since I jerked him off. I really do think that was the original thing they wanted to see happen. Hell — maybe they should have just told me what they wanted! Knowing me back then, if they'd have given me another five bucks, I'm sure I would have stuck it in his mouth! Hey, knowing now how those guys liked to look at it all the time, maybe I could have made some money by charging them to either look at it or maybe touch it! Shit man, maybe I missed out on a good thing!"

"Oh God Bob! Keep talking man! Keep talking, you are getting this guy all crazy and sexy. I've got to hear this, and then I want us to find some secret corner someplace where you can make me a real man! I'm getting real jealous of the things you have done or had done to you! Shit man, I feel left out! Oh man, I never knew this kind of stuff really happened to real guys! Yeah, I guess I really did, but I just never had anybody to talk to about it and hearing somebody tell about it, that really got to do it! When I read about it in the mags, it just sounds so made up! Oh Bob, what did Skip do next?"

"He did my left foot last and then he slowly started up my leg with his tongue. He'd get up to my bag and then he's go down the other leg and then all they way back up it. I was in complete heaven while he was doing this. I had never been treated so heavenly, as what he was doing to me. If somebody had knocked on the door and yelled that the apartment building was on fire, I would have just said, OK! Taking what he was doing for me was a hell of a lot more important than trying to get out of a burning building! Man that felt so damn good to me! After he got done with my legs, then he started sucking on my bag and on my balls! I had never, ever had my balls sucked and chewed on before and I just about went through the roof when he did that! Oh my God! What a feeling! Jim, he'd just put his mouth right up beside my bag and one of the balls, and then he'd suck that ball right into his mouth! Oh shit man, what a great feeling! That was something that I had never even read about and what a great feeling to have it done to you! Right then, I was really sorry I had never let him play with me all of those times when we were in high school and he kept making those suggestions that we go fishing together. I knew damn well back then that fishing was not his objective, and that night is when I decided I had really missed some good fishing days, if I had not been so damn stupid and contrary. I don't know who else he ever played with, so if I had gone with him, I guess it would have been our secret, but I guess I was just too afraid that it would get printed in the local gab sheet that I was out in the woods with the gay guy!"

"He sucked on you, he sucked on you! Tell me about you getting sucked on! Come on man, tell me about it!"

"Oh yeah — he did! Yeah — he sure did! He was one hell of a sucker! I have not been sucked on by that many guys, but I will say that one knew what in the hell he was doing!"

"Bob, sucked on by that many guys? You've been sucked on by more than just this Skip guy?"

"Oh, did I say that — well, —yeah, a few more. But I will say, none of them could suck like Skippy! I'll tell you about those guys later. They were no big deal! Well yeah, maybe one of them, —the one that did me in the men's room of a police station in Texas once. I guess maybe he might have been a big deal! The real funny situation of how it happened, is what made that one real exciting! Met him while I was eating dinner at a counter in a diner, and we started talking and he got real inquisitive and after some period of time, he told me he really did want me to follow him to the police station, where we could use the men's room. Hell, I was horny and he was the one that managed to get the subject onto sex! He was the little town's cop, so I figured, why not? The cop wanted to suck me off! He told me that right there in the diner! That was all there was to it. Guess he found his dicks to suck on, that way! Meet 'em at the diner and take 'em back to the station and use the restroom! Only time I ever got sucked off in a police station! Anyway, back to Skip, and his mouth on my dick! Damn man, that was good! I went over to his place thinking that I was just there to get my ass fucked, but I guess Skip knew right up front, that you just don't let a guy in your house and immediately slam your dick up in his ass. He took hold of my dick, looked at it, licked the sides of it, put just the very tip of it in his mouth and sucked real hard-on it. I could feel his tongue rolling around the edge of it, and I could feel him actually making love to the tip of it, and then all of a sudden, he threw his head back, he opened his mouth as wide as he could and he threw his head down on me and took the entire thing down in his throat. He did that so damn fast I did not know what was happening until it was over. I almost shit! I had no idea that a guy could take a dick down into his throat like he did. I thought that when a guy got a blowjob, it was just the end of his dick like he was doing on the tip of mine. I never knew that a guy could swallow the whole thing, and yes, I do admit that I know mine is bigger that most guy's dicks are. I'm like all guys. Whenever I'm in a shower room or someplace where guys have no pants on, yeah — I check 'em out too. So far, I'm still standing good, except for two black guys that used to be at State with me that I happened to see, all by accident. Another one of those times when a person just happens to walk in at a very inappropriate time. Of course when I did see, what I did happen to see, I wished I had handled it a lot different, so that I could have been part of their party, but it was too late then. I tried to tell them that I rather appreciated what I had happened to walk in on, but I guess they just were not in the mood to accept some little white guy, and his short little white cock, into their cock measuring contest."

"Oh you telling me that what I've always heard is right — black guys do have bigger dicks, is that right?"

"Well, from those two I saw that day, it they are anyplace close to average, hell yes!"

"Damn man, I've always heard that, but course, never got to see for myself! But hey, back to Skip and you! He's sucking on you! Right?"

"Oh yeah — back to Skip and his sucking! Yeah Jim, he took all of it and he kept coming back for more every time he had to come up for air. A couple of times he'd pull off of it and say,' Damn man, I have wanted this, and I am finally getting it! Thanks man, thanks!' Shit man I was probably there, in his living room for more than an hour, just getting my dick sucked on and licked on by him before he finally took me by the hand and said, 'Hey, let's go to the bedroom.' By this time, I guess I had lost all my nervousness. I was anxious as hell to get in that room and lay down. Once again all I could think about was that guy in the drunk tank and how he liked having that great big burly guy's dick up in his ass. I figured that if some great big guy, like that log cutter, or whatever he was, could feel that good up inside of you, then a normal sized guy had to feel good too. I was ready for getting it, and I was wanting it — then! Right then! And the funny thing that I kept thinking about was — thank goodness this is not in a jail drunk tank, and not some big fat drunk guy, like the one that did the fucking in the jail house that night."

"Oh my God man, shit! Keep going man, keep going! I gotta hear bout you and Skip and what he did to you!"

"We got into the bedroom, and Skip told me to just lie down on the bed, on my gut. He took some lube, which I did find out later is kind of a necessity when getting fucked, and rubbed some of it on his dick, and then pushed some of it up in my butt. As soon as he did that, I knew, rather instinctively, that some slick stuff back there had to be used, but then I remembered how the guys in the jail never used anything. I figured that since they both were so drunk, that either the little guy had already been fucked that night and still had a greasy asshole, or neither one of them could feel it, even if it did feel kind of dry. Hell, his insides could have been ripped and torn and he probably never felt it, the way he was feeling that night!"

"I laid there and spread my arms and my legs. As soon as I did that, I wondered if maybe that was not a natural invitation of, "Use me, fuck me!" Skip did not tell me to spread out, I just did it! I laid there and felt him lay down on top of me. He told me to relax, and that everything would be OK. By that time, he didn't need to tell me to relax. I was completely relaxed, even though I was just about to get a dick pushed up inside of my ass for the first time! I guess I knew everything was OK and my ass was ready for it, since I was about ready to beg him to hurry up and fuck me. I'm sure that any normal guy that gets it up in the ass for the first time has to be a hell of a lot more nervous and anxious about what is going to happen back there, than I was that night! I had fingered myself before, but I had never had a dick pushed up in there, and I know I should have been nervous, but I just wasn't! Like I said, all I could think about was that little guy in the drunk tank and him asking for more, once the big guy got off of him. That big guy and the dick that I saw hanging from him when he got off of that little guy, had to have made that little guy awfully full up inside. I figured, if he liked it, then I could too! Yeah, I know I was drunk that night too, or I would not have been in there, but I'm a little afraid that if that big drunk guy would have laid down on top of me, I would have let him do me, once I saw that other guy get it. I guess I'm glad he didn't even see me, or want me anyway!"

"Oh God Bob, are you sure you would have let that guy up in you? He didn't sound like too good of a type to be getting fucked by, don't you think?"

"Yeah, I definitely do agree, but you've got to remember, I was drunk that night too! Being drunk will make a person do some funny stuff. But thank goodness I didn't get fucked by him, and I'm glad now! Yeah, imagine some big old fat, smelly, drunk, guy poking his dick up in your ass! Skip was my first fuck and I'm glad for that!"

"Your FIRST fuck!? I guess what you are telling me is that Skip was not your first and your last fuck—right?"

"Oh yeah! Guess I had better be a little more careful how I phrase some of the stuff or you are going to know way more about me than I planned on sharing! But shit man, I'm not so sure there's anything more about me that I can tell. Telling you about my gay sex stuff is about as far as a guy can go, I think! But—back to Skip —I was on the bed, on my gut. I was all spread out like an Eagle in flight. Skip had lubed me and his dick up. He kept telling me to just relax, that everything was going to be OK. I was about to tell him that if he didn't hurry up and put that big stick of his up in my ass, then things were not going to be OK. He just did not know how anxious I was to feel a dick up in me. Finally, and I do mean finally, he aimed the tip of his dick at my rose bud, in other words my asshole! I could feel it right at the edge. I actually yelled, "Fuck me! Fuck me!" I guess all of sudden, or because of the yelling, Skip decided that I wanted to get fucked and I was anxious for it! I heard him say, "Hang on" and all of a sudden my ass was full of dick! Yeah, it did hurt right at first, but I guess I did not care. I started humping my ass up and down trying to fuck myself with his dick. He caught on pretty quickly and then started fucking me like a real pro. All I can remember is he kept telling me that he just knew I had been fucked before. He kept telling me that no guy ever gets fucked this hard the first time he gets it up in the ass. I kept trying to tell him that I had never been fucked before, but he kept telling me that he just knew I had been fucked before. He kept telling me that no guy ever wants it that fast, or that hard, if he has never been fucked before. I never did convince him that was my first time getting fucked. He fucked me for about 45 minutes or so, and when we finally did get done, he was still making comments about wondering just how many times I had been fucked in the ass before and how big was the biggest dick I had ever taken. I just simply could not convince him that his dick was the only dick I had ever had up in me! I guess paying him a strong complement in letting him know that he really did make a first time fuckee a very happy guy, just did not fit. He just refused to think that he could do a new ass, as hard and as roughly as I had taken it and actually have it be that guy's first fucking. I do agree with one statement he had made earlier at the coffee shop, though! Yes, I definitely was glad, I had done it, once it was over. In fact, I was very glad! Fact is, I was damn glad I was doing it even before it was over. I had been wanting to do that ever since that night when I saw that guy get fucked in the jail, and it had finally happened! I had been fucked, and I was glad! I finally knew what something more than just my fingers felt like up in my ass. It felt good, and I liked it. That's when I truly understood why guys, even some straight guys, find gay guys to fuck their asses once in awhile. It's something that a woman just can't do for you, but something that is worth getting done whenever the times and events happen just right for it! Jim, it's been quite awhile since I've had some guy up in there, and I'm hoping maybe you'll be the next one to use me. I've been thinking about getting you to fuck me for a long time now, and I'm finally letting you know what I want! Jim, I want you to fuck me, and I wanna fuck you, if you'll let me! Can I? OK? You game?"

Chapter Two: Pizza Delivery

"Oh shit man, God, how in the hell can I say no after the way you have me all steamed up? Well, anyway, me fucking your ass! I'm all for that — but I gotta think about maybe letting you fuck me! Bob there is no way in hell that I ever dreamt of maybe you being interested in playing with guys, and yeah, I do have to admit that when we are in the pool together and kind of rubbing up against each other, it does give me a hard-on, but I sure did not think I could let you know that. Bob, I've wanted to play with some guy, any guy, for years now, but I just never had any opportunity, where I could let it happen. Right now, I am "riding high" with knowing that you can understand my feelings and that I will finally get to do some stuff. Bob, I've never done anything like this before, so you've got to understand that I am going to be damn nervous and won't know what to do, so you are gonna have to give me instructions. OK? I'm willing — Oh hell, yes, I'm more than willing — but I'm scared man! God man! Right now I feel like I'm some ten or twelve year old kid doing stuff that he really knows is wrong, but still wanting to do, just to find out about it! You know how they talk about kids doing some funny stuff to each other, 'out behind the barn,' well that sure is the way I'm feeling right now! It's kind of like knowing that older people do it, so I want to do it too! God, I feel like some little kid, right now!"

Jim there really isn't anything to be scared about! Yeah, I really do want to fuck you if I can! Trust me, I've done it — I've gotten fucked — I've been fucked in the ass, and if there was anything to be afraid of, I wouldn't be asking you to do it. I really do want you to fuck me, and I'm hoping I can fuck you then! I sure wouldn't be telling you it feels good, if it didn't! You said you've been wanting to do something for a long time. Jim, this is your chance! I'm giving you an ass, to fuck! I really wanna do it! When did you first start thinking about doing something? What got you to thinking that way?"

"Well Bob, I guess it's, kind of, almost like you watching the two guys fucking in the drunk tank. When I was just a kid back home, I delivered papers. I was probably about 13 or 14 years old, and I had to get off of my bike at some of the places and walk the paper up to someplace special, rather than just throw it toward the house. Well anyway, there was this one house, sat out all by itself some, no other houses real close to it, and that was one of the places where I had to walk it up to the house, instead of just throwing it. The dogs around there liked to get the paper and chew it up, so I took it up and put it on a shelf where the dogs that ran loose around there couldn't get it. Two guys lived in that house. Hey, I was young and really stupid and did not even know that gays existed. To me two guys living together was no big deal. They were kind of middle aged, well probably like our age now, but to me, back then, anybody over about 25 was middle aged. So anyway I never thought anything about them living there together. I delivered the morning paper, another kid delivered the evening paper. That was a different newspaper company. Well, like I said, at this one house — they were Al and Richard, I always walked up to the front of the house and put the paper on the shelf. One really nice Sunday spring morning, one of the very first warm days we had that year, I walked up to the porch to put the paper on the shelf and their front door was standing open. They were both lying on the floor, on top of some sleeping bags, totally naked. They were sound asleep, but the Richard guy was lying on his side and he had his arm over Al's chest. I could see Al's dick, and I will tell you that until that time I did not know a man's dick got bigger when he got older. Dad never, ever, went without pants on, and I had never seen a grown man's dick before. Bob, he was still asleep, but he was laying there on his back, with a raging morning hard-on, and that damn thing was just way too big to be part of him! I stood there on the front porch and just stared at that dick! To me it looked like a big fucking cucumber stuck to his body. Damn it looked big! It made me reach down and rub my own little peter! I must have stood there of at least three or four minutes just looking in their front door! I was in shock at, number one, seeing Al's big hard-on dick, and number two, seeing those two guys laying there totally naked and kind of hugging each other. That was something I had just never thought about happening before."

"Oh shit man! What a way to find out about real life!"

"God, yeah man! Bob, I did not know what to do. I wanted to just stand there and stare, but I kept looking back to see if anybody could see me looking in their door. I don't think anybody saw me — that I know of, anyway!"

"Well, what did you do man? What happened?"

"I dropped the damn newspaper! I was just standing there and I totally forgot I had their newspaper in my hand. It was the Sunday paper, and they were always a lot bigger and thicker than the other days. When it hit the floor, it made a thud! Richard jumped and looked at the door. I ran! I ran back to my bike and I peddled my ass out of there as fast as I could! I don't know why, but for some stupid reason I must have thought they were chasing me or something. I delivered the rest of my papers that morning faster than I had ever done before!"

"Shit man! What ever happened after that? Did you talk to Richard and Al after that, or what ever happened? I mean, you still had to deliver their paper, right?"

"Yeah, I did, but I got up to the porch and got it on the shelf real quickly, and then got out of there. I don't know why, but I felt like I shouldn't be there anymore. I really didn't do anything real wrong, I mean they were the ones lying there completely naked. Hell anybody could have come up to that door and seen 'em lying there. It just happened to me, though."

"So Jim, like later — I'm sure you must have talked to them when you collected or sometime, right?"

"Yeah, about two weeks later I did have to go collect and I was scared. I don't know what I expected to have happen, or for them to say, but I was scared. I hadn't told anybody, and I do mean anybody of what I saw that day. Seriously that big dick on Al was way too much for me to even think could be real. Bob, to me he looked like a horse laying there on his back. Man, I kind of wanted to tell a friend of mine about it, but I really did think he would call me a fibber if I tried to tell him about the size of that dick. See none of us young kids had ever seen a grown man's dick, let alone a hard-on, I'm sure. I mean, all the other kids lived in real uptight households like I did. Hell, we had big baggy swim trunks to wear. Our families were very modest! Like your Speedos — hell man, nobody around me would ever wear anything that sexy! No way!"

"So Jim, back to your story, what happened when you did talk to Al and Richard?"

"Oh, well I knocked on their door and once again it was standing open. It was just the screen door that was closed. Just like that Sunday morning. Anyway, Richard came to the door. He invited me in, and right then I was not so sure I really wanted to go in. He paid me, then he said, — 'Hey Jimmy, I kind of think maybe we kind of scared you the other morning when you dropped the paper on the floor, didn't we?' I kind of just said, 'Yeah.' Then he said that when they went to sleep the night before they never thought about me coming up onto the porch to put the paper there. He said they had wanted to sleep there on the floor since the spring breeze felt so good, and they did not mean to scare me or anything. Then he asked me why I ran away so fast when he looked up. I told him I was kind of scared, and that I thought maybe I should not have seen in through the door. Then he asked me if I understood that he and Al were like married people. I kind of uttered some kind of a yeah, but I really did not understand what he meant! To me this was still way too weird! Anyway, he then told me that they would try and be more careful about being in there without any clothes on when they knew I would be coming up on the porch. I just kind of answered, 'OK,' then I turned around and left. After that, I never saw either one of them naked again, but they did kind of act a little more friendly toward me, like for some reason we had some kind of an un-stated understanding between us. Bob, I've got to admit, that from that Sunday morning on, I started looking at guys' crotches a whole lot more than I had ever done before. Hell man, before that morning, a guy's crotch was of no interest. Hell man, we were all just little kids. None of us had any dicks to talk about, but shit man, I had finally seen something that I never expected to see! After that day, I really did wonder if all guys' dicks got that big, and when I started getting bigger myself, then I really started watching and trying to see what other guys had. I guess that's what made me start to wonder about guys, and made me want to do something with someone. I've still got that image in my mind of that great big long stiff dick standing straight up in the air that morning! I just never knew a guy's dick could ever get that big, or that stiff! Shit man, what a life-changing day that morning was! I knew I didn't understand everything that I had seen that day, but I sure did know I had seen something that none of by buddies had seen. After that, every chance I got to try and check out some guy's dick, in like maybe the shower room at school, I did. I wanted to see if some of the older guys were getting bigger dicks as they got older, and I sure as the hell was hoping that they did, so that mine would finally get bigger some day too."

"Well, it finally did, didn't it?"

"Yeah, it finally did, but I sure was impatient waiting on it to do it. After talking to Richard and not feeling quite so scared about being out by their house, I prayed every time I went out there that I'd get to see one of them naked again. I really did want to see one of them running around inside with nothing on! I wanted to see their dicks and their butts! Never did! They were always really nice to me, but nothing else ever happened. You know Bob, now that I'm older and my dick had finally grown up some, I wonder if I were to see that Al's dick all over again, I wonder if now I'd think it was that damn big, or if now, I'd just kind of look at it as being normal? I do know though, that day, I thought I had seen the biggest dick on some guy that any man could have. I thought that guy was built way out of proportion. I really do wish I could have had some way to measure it, or compare it to something, just so I could know now, if it was really a lot bigger than normal."

"Hey interesting thought Jim — interesting! Yeah I wonder too! You know how when we are little kids, some things just look a whole lot bigger then, than they do later. But, you've got to remember, you had never seen some grown man's rod before, and the very first time you get to see one, it's a total boner standing straight up in the air! Hell man, I'll bet that would have shook me too!"

"Well, anyway Bob, you were wondering when I started getting interested in other guys, and that is the when. Been years and years ago, and now today is the very first time that I've been with some guy that I can be open with. You asked me earlier if you could fuck my ass, and I never really said — 'Yes, hell yes!' Got to admit that the idea of getting it up in the ass has never really been one of my main desires, but Bob, after you telling me about those guys in the jug and that little guy getting fucked in the ass, and then your experiences and how you like it so much, sure, I'm game! I fully trust you man, and I've got to admit there is nobody else that I'd like to know is up in there, poking around, other than you."

Then looking all around, Jim asked, "Where we going to do this? Out here or in the house? Nobody can see in this yard from anyplace can they?"

"No, nobody can see in, unless an airplane flies over, but I think I'd feel more comfortable if we were in the house. And I'll tell you that I really do think we had better order that pizza before we get started or we might loose track of time, and then the gals will be home and they will be asking why we never ordered a pizza."

"Oh yeah, I think you are right! Yeah, I agree. If we get started and then it gets too late, we could be in some real deep shit. Yeah, let's order it, and then it will be here for us to eat whenever we get around to it."

"OK! Let's do!" Bob replied. "Hey, is that deluxe pizza from down at the Corner Pizza Shop good for you?"

"Yeah, that sounds great to me. You going to order it and have it delivered or are we going to go down for it?"

"No, I'll call and order it. We order from there quite often and they deliver here all the time. I'll be right back. I'm going in to order it and I'll be right back!"

Jim swam in the pool a couple of length while Bob was in the house and on the phone, and he then came back out to the pool area.

"It's ordered. They said it would take about 30 minutes, so I guess maybe we had better keep at least a towel on us since I don't know who will be delivering it. I told Sam, the guy on the phone, that if one of the normal delivery guys deliver it, to tell them to just come in through the side gate since we were out back and would not hear the doorbell. He said that he thought all three of the guys that are working today had delivered here before. So, anyway, some guy will be coming in pretty soon."

Bob and Jim did some more swimming, in the nude, until Bob suggested that maybe they needed to get out of the pool and get some trunks on so that they were ready for the delivery guy. As they both got out of the pool, Bob put his Speedos on, and Jim just wrapped a towel around himself.

Jim looked at Bob's crowded crotch, and the bulge that was definitely showing since he of course did have a major hard-on. As they had been during their entire time in the water, they had been playing with each other just before they got out of the pool. Bob's towel was not exactly hanging straight down either!

Jim looked at Bob's manly, hunky, appearance and reached out and put his hand right on Bob's crotch. He squeezed and he grinned. "Oh man, that is so nice! Bob that is such a nice, nice dick man!"

Bob grinned back at Jim, put his hand around Jim's neck and pulled him forward and gave him a hug and groped his crotch also. "This one's pretty damn nice too man! Pretty damn nice!"

As they stood there with Jim's hand definitely feeling the material of Bob's Speedos being stretched to its fullest, and with Bob's left hand on Jim's crotch, his face lying on Jim's shoulder and his right hand now reaching around and sliding his hand up between the butt cheeks that were not so completely covered, Bob quietly said, "Oh man! In just a little while I am going to get to slide my dick up in here where my fingers are right now. Oh Jim, I have wanted to fuck that ass ever since the first time I saw it! Oh man, I finally get to fuck it today! I can't wait!"

"Excuse me gentlemen! I have your pizza here!"

All of a sudden Bob and Jim realized that they were no longer alone in the back yard. Bob spun around and almost yelled, "Oh my God! How long have you been standing there?"

"Just a couple of minutes, but maybe long enough to know your wives are not here today, are they?"

Bob again stuttered and tried to talk, but he was all shook that he had been caught rather kissing Jim's neck and also feeling up his ass and definitely groping his crotch!

"Cool man, cool!" The pizza driver said. "It's all cool men, it's all cool! I've seen a lot more than this before, believe me, and besides, I like what I'm seeing!"

"When in the hell did you come in?" Bob excitedly asked. "I did not hear you open the gate or anything! What are you driving? I never even heard a car or anything! When did you come in?"

"Hey Mr. Southers, don't worry about it! I like to do things kind of quietly because when I do, then I get to see stuff like this, and this is definitely the best I've seen for a long time! You would be surprised how often I can just happen to come up upon something like this, if I work real quietly. And right now, I am happier about what I have just found, than I have been in a long time!"

The driver sat the pizza down on the patio table, licked his lips, kind of rubbed his hands together a little, and without saying another word, moved over a little closer to Bob and Jim, and then reached up under Jim's towel and grabbed his hard-on with his left hand, and at the same time, slid his right hand down into the front of Bob's Speedos.

Looking at both men and their worried expressions on their faces, Cole just simply said, "See men, no problem at all! We're all in this together. I want both of you! God, you both feel great!"

Bob and Jim simply stood there in complete shock and surprise at Cole's straightforward actions. He expressed no hesitation in going for what he wanted to feel and grab. All of his actions were as if this happened all of the time. He knew he now had two, really hot looking and built men, that were "into it", and he was gonna take advantage of it! Totally normal actions — as far as he was concerned.

"I've delivered pizzas here before, but your wives were always here then. I was hoping for a day like this! I knew it would happen some day if I was patient! I've seen both of you guys sporting hard-ons when you came to the door to get the pizzas. And it always happened when you two were both here! Damn man, today is finally the day I've been waiting on! Hey guys, I'm Cole. My name is Cole."

Then looking at Bob, he asked, "Mr. Southers, what is your first name?"

"It's Bob. Bob Southers!"

Then turning toward Jim, Cole then added, "And I know your last name is Taddem, but what is your first name?"

Jim looked at Cole and replied. Jim, it's Jim but how do you know my last name? How do you know that?"

"Men, in my business, it pays to know who orders and who's getting pizzas! They know down at the shop that I have my special customers that I insist I get to deliver to, if I'm there, and of course you two are definitely on the top of that list! I just knew that if I was patient, some day like this would finally come! You both feel real good! You guys have got nice dicks. I'll bet you two really have fun together, don't you? Hey, where are the women today men? Just here playing with each other and no women around today?"

Unconsciously Bob had put his hand onto Coles' waist as they stood there, and Bob had done the same thing, but he neither realized what he had done. When Cole "moved in" and slid his hand down Bob's Speedos, and up and under Jim's towel, that definitely made it a close, small grouping. All three men were body touching, with just standing there. Appreciating the statements that everything was cool, as Cole put it, Bob started feeling a little less panicked, and he kind of explained that their wives had gone to a dinner and a movie.

"Oh wow!" Cole exclaimed! "That means they are going to be gone for quite awhile, right?"

"Yeah." Bob answered. Yeah, till later tonight!"

"Good!" Cole exclaimed. "Hey men, I want to be part of your playing, can I?"

Bob took a deep breath and asked, "What? What did you just say?"

Cole grabbed hold of Bob's dick and repeated, "I want to be part of your playing, can I? Men, I have prayed for this day ever since I've been delivering to your houses! Don't tell me no, please!"

Bob looked at Jim! Jim looked back at Bob and just kind of slowly shook his head, expressing, "I can't believe this man! I just can't believe this!"

Bob looked at Cole and asked, "Cole, how old are you? Do you play with guys all the time?"

"Hey don't worry men! I'm old enough! I'm 22 and I'm definitely not a virgin. Yeah, I play with guys all the time, all kinds of guys, and getting to play with two that look like you two, is a real feather in my cap! You guys, —both of you guys, are hot as hell and I have prayed for this day to happen to me, for as long as I've known either one of you. Both of you guys are just the type that gay guys want to get in the sack, all the time! You are both hot as hell! Please let me play! I've been wanting either one of you, and getting both of you at the same time is heaven man, real heaven!"

"Well Cole, what about your deliveries? Don't you have some work to do? Isn't the shop expecting you back?"

"Hey no problem! We are definitely not busy today, and all I need to do is call and tell Sam to let Dave and Joey take care of the rest of the night, and he won't care. Dave and Joey will be glad because they'll get more tips that way too. They'll be happy! Please guys, please?"

"Cole is your Pizza truck parked outside? I mean, I really don't want the neighbors asking Judy why the pizza guy was here for so long."

"Hey man, like I said before. In my business, it pays to know who orders and who's getting pizzas! When I found out just where this pizza was going to, the ole pizza truck stayed there. I just had this funny feeling that today was going to finally be my pay off day, and I drove my own car, just so that if I did get to let it sit there for awhile, nobody would notice. Finally I played my cards right!"

Standing there, all in a group hug, and of course with Cole's hands still down into Bob's trunks, and up under Jim's towel, Bob and Jim did, finally, agree that Cole could stay for just a little while, and they emphasized — a little while, since they definitely were kind of all up tight about even the two of them playing, and just praying that the wives did not come home early for some funny reason.

As Cole continued to enjoy the feeling of Bob's enormous rod stuffed into his Speedos, and also managing to slide a "not un-noticed" finger up into Jim's virgin ass crack, Bob and Jim quickly explained how this was their first time of playing together, and this was, in-fact, Jim's fist time of doing anything with any guy.

Jim felt his ass being played with, he knew he had a finger stuck up in there, he liked it, and he managed to slightly move even closer to Cole so that he could penetrate even further!

As Cole pushed his finger up into Jim's ass as far as he could, he also managed to unleash Bob's stick of meat, and get it out of the top of his Speedos. While still finger fucking Jim, he jerked and played with Bob's, now exposed, dick.

"Oh shit man!" Cole exclaimed. "God men, this is going to be great! I never imagined that you two were not into playing with each other as often as possible. Really guys, I figured you two were doing each other all the time. That's one of the reasons I was so damn sure that this kind of a day would finally happen — if I was just patient!"

"OK here's the deal man!" Bob said as he looked at Cole, as Cole was still jerking him off. "We are going to go inside and you get to suck on each of us, and then you have to get out of here! I know they're not supposed to be home until about 10 or so, but the idea of having some pizza delivery guy still here when they get home, at whatever time that is, just would not be good! OK, you agree?"

"Hey man, I totally agree! Give me 20 minutes — 10 minutes on each of you guys and I will be out of here. Sure not as long as I was hoping for, but to get to taste both of you two, I'll do whatever you say! Besides, before I leave, you two guys are going to have my address and my phone number, and you are then going to have your own very private play space that you can use, whenever you guys need it! I know both of you guys, and I can trust both of you with everything I have, so you guys are going to end up with a safe place by using my apartment whenever you need it! OK?"

"OK? You ask? —OK?" Bob exclaimed! "Hell yes man! God that would be great wouldn't it Jim? Shit man! I never expected this much out of a pizza delivery guy before! God man, you really deliver, don't you? Shit man, I hope I have been tipping you enough! God, that is great! Cole, get your hand out of my trunks and out of Jim's ass, grab that pizza, and let's get inside!"

Chapter Three: In The Kitchen

"Cole just put that pizza on the table over there. And remember, you said 10 minutes on each of us and you'd be out of here in 20 minutes, right?" Bob asked. He was experiencing some nervousness of having the delivery guy, Cole, there in the house. When he knew it would be just Jim and himself, he did not feel this concerned, but having the third person there was not feeling too comfortable.

"Yeah, Jim, just let me have the 20 minutes and I promise to be gone. Just the idea of finally getting to be with both of you guys is enough to make me do whatever you want. I've been waiting for this day to happen for so long I'm not going to screw it up now! Hey Jim, take your Speedos off and you two guys stand there beside each other and I'm going to do some cock sucking and cock servicing. I'm gonna kind of do both of you at the same time."

Jim and Bob stood beside the kitchen counter and both proudly displayed and presented their raging hard-ons to Cole for his sucking and licking pleasures. Cole grabbed a hold of Jim's bag as he turned his face toward Bob, and immediately sucked all of Bob's rod into his throat.

"Oh my God man, oh man, that feels so good!" Bob exclaimed. "Yeah man, yeah suck it, suck it hard!"

Jim stood there with his bag and his dick firmly planted in Cole's hand, and watched Jim's dick completely disappear down into Cole's throat.

Suddenly Cole pulled off of Bob's meat and almost without Jim realizing what was happening, Cole had fully taken all of Jim's cock!

"Oh shit man, oh shit! Oh man that feels good!" Jim rather squealed! Oh man that is good! Yeah man, yeah, suck it, suck it hard! Oh Bob, he feels so good! Oh shit man, that is great! God man, you gotta remember I've never had some guy sucking on my dick before! Shit man, this is good!"

Just as suddenly as Cole had moved over to Jim and took him fully, he switched back and again took Bob's meat. For the entire 20 minutes that the two men had told Cole he could be there, he used both men fast and furiously. He'd suck on Bob's cock for a minute, then he'd pull his cock up and out of the way and suck both of Bob's balls into his mouth, and then do the same thing to Jim and his nuts. Both men were expressing their pleasure and excitement in the fantastic way that Cole was treating them.

Bob even admitted that he had never had his balls sucked on quite like that! "Chew my balls man, chew my balls! Oh Cole, yeah, I like you on my balls! Yeah man, I like that, do that! Bite 'em man, bite 'em!"

As Cole used the meat sticks and sucked on the balls, that he had been wanting for so long, Jim and Bob explored and discovered the great feelings of being able to openly touch and feel the other man. It had become quite apparent that Jim was now much more comfortable with this action, than he had been earlier. Bob could tell from Jim's actions that he was definitely enjoying this action, and he was eagerly participating. Bob was gently pinching Jim's nipples, and he was getting a very good reaction! He could even see Jim's hard-on flip up higher whenever he pinched a tit, even, ever so slightly!

Suddenly Cole stood up and said, "Guys, my 20 minutes are up, and I'm out of here! I don't want to be, but, we had a deal and I'm standing up to my part of it, cause I want both of you guys to trust me, and know that I do what I say I'll do.

Cole grabbed some paper from his delivery pad, and wrote his address and his cell phone number on it, twice, and handed it to each of the men.

"Hey guys, at the front door is a table with flower pots. Pick up the red pot, the one with the fake flowers in it, and you'll find the front door key. Use my place anytime you guys need a place, and of course, use me for whenever I can make up for a missing person. In other words — I'm always eager and anxious to fill in if it happens that just one of you is available. I've got guys coming and going out of that place all the time, so hey, maybe you'll happen to find a couple more guys that you want to play with too! Don't know if you'll be interested or not, but I do happen to deliver pizzas to the State Highway Patrol office every Friday night, so as it so happens, I've gotten to know a couple of those guys, and they kind of like using my place, secretively, too. So anyway, you just might have to share a bed sometime if too many guys all show up at the same time. I've never had too many all show up at the same time — yet — but I'm still hoping! Now — when can the three of us get together over there and let me really get down to business with you two? Today was just a preview of what's gonna happen. I've been begging for this day ever since I delivered the first pizza to either one of your houses and saw just one of you. Then when I saw the other one, seriously man, I assumed you two were taking care of each other all the time. Seriously man, whenever I saw you two together, I'd swear the one that I talked to looked like he had a hard-on. Hey, with the size you've got though, maybe you just look like you have a hard-on all the time!" He said as he looked back down at Bob's meat. "Anyway, it's about time you two finally got to it! And thank goodness, you ordered a pizza today!"

After a very quick discussion, the three men agreed that the following Thursday night, at about 8PM, when Bob and Jim were "supposed" to go bowling together, would be the best time to aim for, as far as the three of them getting together!

Cole then quickly exited through the kitchen door, and left the two hunky neighbors standing there, in the middle of the kitchen, fully nude, in each other's arms, and still sporting major hard-ons.

Jim looked at Bob, Bob returned the look and each simply smiled!

"Bob, I can't believe this! Come on man, I need to cool off in the pool. Let's jump in."

"OK, sounds like a plan. Hey, I'm gonna bring this pizza out — uh Jim — Jim, we never paid for the pizza! He never got paid!"

"Oh shit man! Hey, I kind of guess we might have had our minds on other things! He never mentioned it did he?"

"No he didn't!" Supposed he didn't intend to get paid once he found us out there feeling each other up?"

"I don't know, I really have no idea! Next Thursday night when we see him, then we'll pay him. He sure doesn't need to pay for our pizza. Course, maybe he's just figuring that's the price he pays for getting to suck on two such good looking cocks?"

Jim looked back toward Bob, spread a big grin across his face, due to Bob's comment about the 'two good looking cocks', and said, "Hey, the way he goes after cock, if he's not collecting for the pizzas, he probably pays the pizza shop more than he earns. You know what!? I'm glad he caught us, I really am! Look! With him finding us in action, we gained a private place we can use whenever we want. Sounded like to me — that we can just stop in anytime we want, right? Is that what you gathered?"

"Yeah, but what happens if we're in there fucking around and he comes home? Then what?"

"I don't know, wonder if he thought of that!"

"I don't know either — guess maybe we just might find out sometime! That should be fun! Hey, that's probably what he wants to have happen! Cops? He has some state cops come by? Hey man, this is getting better all the time!"

"Hey Bob, come on, let's take this pizza out back and hit the pool. OK?"

Bob and Jim each safely put away the note that Cole had given each of them, took a moment or two to, both, have a good laugh over the fact that even though they had both been very nicely sucked on by Cole, neither one of them knew what kind of equipment Cole was packing.

"Shit man!" Jim rather shakily expressed. "Neither one of us told him to drop his pants so we could see what he had! God, were we self-centered, or what? Hell, neither one of us has any idea at all what he's packing in those pants of his! It might be a foot long dog, as far as we know!"

After their embarrassed concern that neither one of them had even asked Cole to drop his pants so they could see his stick of meat, they went back out to the pool area and after putting the pizza and a couple of beers on the table, jumped into the pool.

"Oh Bob, I can't believe this! I sure as hell never expected this day to turn out anything like this! Let alone, our finally, just sharing experiences with each other is way beyond belief, but our actual doing some stuff together is way more than I can even imagine happening!"

And, having said that, Jim reached over and grabbed Bob by the dick. "Man, never thought I'd ever get to do this! Come here man, sit up here on the edge of the pool. I'm finally ready and willing to just see what sucking on some guy's dick is like. The way Cole was using both of us in there sure has convinced me it's gotta be, as they say, 'It's gotta be a good thing.' Come on man, it's time for me to do it, let me get you!"

Looking at Jim, Bob let out a very big grin, and then jumped up on the edge of the pool, moved down into the more shallow end of the pool where Jim could stand on the bottom and put his face right in Bob's crotch.

Jim moved in between Bob's legs, rubbed the outside of each leg, looked up at Bob with somewhat of an, "Oh my God man, I can't believe I'm gonna do this" look, and then actually said it out loud. "Oh my God man, I can't believe I'm gonna do this!"

Silently and without saying anything Bob reached forward and softly rubbed the side of Jim's face and then very slightly suggested, with the movement of his hands, that Jim start leaning forward.

Slowly and with hesitation, Jim started to move his face down toward Bob's stiff and firm hard-on, which was pointing directly at him. He took a very deep breath, opened his mouth widely, and placed it on the tip of Bob's rod! Slowly, he moved his face lower and managed to take more and more of the meat into his mouth.

Bob continued to hold the side of Jim's head and encouraged him to take more and more of his dick, as he could manage.

"Oh yeah Jim, oh yeah! Yeah man, that is great! Oh man I cannot believe it! We are finally sucking on each other. Well — anyway you know what I mean! Yeah man, suck me, suck me!"

Jim managed to take all of Bob's dick down into his throat, and a couple of times, even forced his face deeply into Bob's crotch, as if to get even more dick, if there was any more to go for.

As Bob grabbed a hold of the sides of Jim's head tighter and pulled him forward, he let out, "Oh shit yes man! God yeah Jim, suck me!"

Slowly Jim got into the sucking in and then a pulling back rhythm, which totally and completely turned Bob on.

"Hey man, put your legs up in the air! Let me at your nuts. Let me see if I can make them feel good like Cole did!" Realizing and learning from what had just happened in the house, Jim sucked on Bob's nuts and let them slip into and out of his mouth! As he let them slide back out, he slightly licked his buddy — back by his asshole! He'd lick some, then chew and sucked on Bob's nuts for a little while, then he'd go back after the cock. For a first timer, he was looking and acting like a pro.

"Oh Jim, oh Jim! Pull off man, pull off! Jim, I'm gonna cum, pull off!"

Jim did, since right then he was not too sure he really was ready to eat Bob's cum, and from the sound of Bob's voice he knew he needed to. Just as soon as he managed to pull back and let Bob's dick come free from his mouth, he was immediately hit in the face and neck with three major shots of thick, white, creamy, cum.

"Oh man, I knew I was gonna do that man, I felt it coming. Here Jim, here take this towel. Sorry man, I didn't mean to make you a gummy mess! I'm sorry! But oh shit man! Your tongue down there under my nuts was driving me crazy! Where in the hell did you learn to do that? Shit man, have you done that to some guys before? God that was hot! Fucking hot! I've never felt that before!"

As Jim took the towel from Bob and started wiping the cum off of his face and his neck, he said to Bob, "Hey man, no need to be sorry! Yeah, I didn't expect it to come flying out at me so fast, but hey, it's on me and not in the pool. Not a problem! Just one of those things that us suckers need to expect I guess!" He stated, laughed and looked at Bob to see his reaction.

"Jim, I can not believe this! I can't believe this!"

Looking up at Bob, Jim asked, "Believe what? What that I sucked you strong enough that you came?"

"No, not that! Jim, I am the one that wanted to get something like this going, I'm the one that started all of this, and now you are the guy that does the first sucking. I still, have never sucked on any guy! Seriously man, I've been fucked, more than once. I've been sucked off more than once. And seriously man, when I told you to drop the towel earlier, so I could see your crotch, I was damn sure then that if any sucking did happen, I would be the one doing it! And now, I still haven't — but yet, you have already sucked me off! Damn man, I want to suck you! Come on! I wanna suck on your dick man, I want it! Get up here and lay down on the lounge chair! This night is not gonna go by now, without me getting to see what sucking on some guy's cock is like! Cole took both of us like we were hanging gold down there, and you sure as the hell didn't have a problem learning damn quick, of what made me feel good, and now I am gonna finally do it to see what in the hell is going on. I'm gonna suck on your dick till you cum, understand? Come here, let me at it!"

Bob rather lead Jim over to the chase lounge and indicated for him to lie down. As Jim did, Bob moved into position and got himself positioned right on top of Jim's rod. With his hands now clasped up behind his head, and his rod standing up at a full attention, Jim calmly laid there and waited for Bob to make "the move."

Moving slowly as if maybe he was having second thoughts about this, Bob slowly started to lower himself down so that his mouth and Jim's, stiffer than usual, hard-on would meet! Jim was allowing Bob to take all the time he needed to finally take it into his mouth, and although slowly and with hesitation, Bob finally did.

"Yeah man, yeah man!" Jim firmly stated as Bob took the first very little tip of it into his mouth! "Yeah, feeling good, feeling good!" Jim encouraged!

Slowly, as if perhaps it might break off, if handled too roughly, Bob managed to sink down lower and lower onto — the first cock he had ever put in his mouth!

"Eat me man, eat me! Come on man, I wanna watch your mouth go down on it!" Jim softly encouraged.

With about one half of the cock length in his mouth, Bob managed to look up at Jim, and saw him smiling broadly at the sight of Bob sucking on his dick. "Eat me man, eat me! Taste me! Suck my dick! Come on buddy, go all the way down, you'll like it!"

Suddenly as if time was running out, Bob actually threw his head down onto Jim's rod so that he had all of it, the entire length in his mouth.

Jim let out with a, "Yeah, man! Yeah, that's the way! That's it! Do it — do it — do it! Oh Bob, that feels so fucking good!"

Jim's verbal excitement of getting his dick fully eaten, definitely got Bob more excited about what he was doing, and he started in some additional actions, the same as if this was normal activity for him. He was now pumping onto Jim's rod and at the same time fingering his asshole.

"Oh yes, oh yes! Oh man stick your finger up in there man, yeah finger fuck my hole! Yeah man, I like that, I like that!" Jim was soundly proclaiming to his hunky neighbor — his close friend neighbor, that now had Jim's dick completely down into his throat and who had his middle finger stuck up into Jim's ass, as far as possible!

Bob was finger fucking Jim as fast as possible, moving his finger in and out, pushing it completely, then pulling it back out, just so he could push it back into the tight little opening, again and again.

"Oh Bob use two fingers, please! Yeah, please poke my hole with your fingers! Oh man, that feels so fucking good! Oh man, I can't wait until you and Cole can use me all at the same time. Yeah, man, yeah! One of you fucking my ass and one of you sucking my cock! Oh Bob, what a night this has turned out to be! Never, never thought about getting to do stuff like this, and especially with you! But God man, oh shit — it is so fucking hot! Suck me man, suck me and finger fuck me!"

With Bob's mouth firmly planted on the entire length of Jim's dick, and his right hand gleefully playing with Jim's asshole, Jim took Bob's left hand and placed it on his right tit and pleaded, "Pinch it man, please pinch my tit!"

As Bob did, Jim then grabbed his own left tit and he tried to even out the great feeling that was now happening to his right tit. He madly pinched his own left tit, to try and get the same feeling of power, that he was getting from Bob pinching his right tit! All of a sudden, he realized for the very first time, that he was actually enjoying pain, as part of this new sexual experience.

For more than half an hour, Jim laid there and let his buddy roam all over him with as much gusto as he could muster. Jim encouraged Bob to get really rambunctious with every part of him that he could feel.

"Oh Bob, oh Bob, I never expected to feel this way! Oh man, I want you to do stuff to me and to my body! Oh man, do it, do it, do it! Suck me, fuck me, pinch me — do me man — do me! Oh Bob, get rough with me! Use me! Play with my body! Make me feel it! Yeah man, yeah! Do it, do it, do it!"

Bob had discovered that all of a sudden he either had found a man that truly wanted and needed mad, wild, sex, or maybe he had just uncovered some of Jim's inner desires that had never been exposed before!

As Jim grabbed both sides of Bob's head and pulled him forward and onto his body as tightly as possible, but only for a second, he started letting Bob know that he was right at a major climax. "Oh shit man!" He exclaimed as he pulled Bob into an inescapable head hold, "Oh shit man, I'm gonna cum — I'm gonna cum! Oh my God man — here it cuummms!"

Almost as if he had thrown Bob's head off and out of the way, Jim let loose with a flood of cum! He shot his Jim juice all over the side of Bob's face, and neck, as well as giving his chest a pretty good coating of semen.

"Oh shit man, oh my God! Wow! Bob, my God man! What a trip! Shit man, you are one fucking hot player! God Bob, I have never felt anything like that before! Oh shit, I can not believe it! God all mighty! Wow! Bob, your mouth sucking on me like a hungry tiger, your fingers stuck up in my asshole and then my tits feeling like there where getting run over by a Mac truck — oh shit man — oh shit! What a fucking great feeling! Wow, you OK? You OK Bob?"

"Yeah, I'm OK if that's what it's called! Yeah! Jim, you turn into a wild beast when you have sex don't you? God man, I thought I was loosing control there for a little while. Man, do you always get that excited and turned on when you have sex? Man, you're into pain when you have sex, aren't you?"

"Oh no man, no! Bob, I have never been that turned on and ragging for more and more like I just was! Yeah, I agree. I'm sure I was acting like some wild beast! Really Bob, I felt like one! Hey man — is that what gay sex is like? I've never associated tit pain with sex before! I mean man, wow — I've been missing out!"

"Jim, I don't know man, this is the first time I've ever been with someone that got that turned on before! Hey really, the only guy I've ever done anything with was that Skip from school, and he sure never got that wild!"

"You know Bob, I think my curiosity that I've carried around with me ever since that day when I saw that big dick on that Al guy, finally came out! Bob, I've got wants and desires in me that I have obviously depressed for a hell of a long time. I've been wanting to do this for a hell of a long time, and I just never allowed myself to go find it and do it! Yeah, I admit now, every time we've been in the pool together and goofing around, yeah, I know now I've always hoped you'd reach out and grab my tits and pinch on them. Man, I just never knew that was really part of having some great sex! Oh man, I like that! Yeah, I've got to admit it — playing around in the pool with you — I always got a major boner. I've had to hide it many of times. I always thought I was pretty good getting it hidden, but I guess not. At least not from you! I wonder if the gals saw it too? Oh fucking shit man, I still feel all hot and bothered! Wow, letting the ole cum fly sure did not turn me off any! Damn man, I wish that Cole guy was back here right now! I wish we could do a three way!"

"Jim gotta tell you — when you mentioned the idea of us two and Cole being together and one of us sucking you off while the other one fucks your butt hole, o'man, o'live — gotta admit that really, really turned me on! I think that's when I got rougher on you! Just the idea of the three of us doing that is way — way too exciting, to even think about! Yeah, I wanna do that!"

"Looking at Bob very suddenly, Jim asked, "I said what? I said I wanted one of you guys to suck me and the other one to fuck me? Is that what you said!?"

"Yeah, yeah, that's what you said you wanted to do! You were wishing Cole was here so one of us could suck you and the other one could fuck you at the same time!"

"Bob, you've gotta be kidding! Bob, I've never been fucked before! Why in the hell would I have said that? Do you think I was saying stuff that I wasn't aware of? Bob, you think I was saying stuff that I really do want, even though I'm still kind of afraid of actually doing it? I don't remember saying that — but if you said I did — then I must have! I know one thing, I'm sure I'd never just tell you or any other guy to pinch the shit out of my tits, but man, during that little session, I sure was wanting something tighter on them than I had! Oh Bob, I think that is really telling me I do want to get fucked, even though the idea of maybe actually doing it is still kind of scary! Wow man, the things I just say without knowing what I'm really thinking and wanting! I do know during that session, I sure was out there far enough, that some good deep thoughts and desires sure could have come out! I think right then, I probably would have been anxious for about six or eight more guys to be involved and doing stuff to me! I was really wanting to be roughed up! That was one fucking hot time! I liked it — yeah I really did!"

"Hey Jim, I think you've already said it! You want fucked, right? I think you need to let me show you how great that can feel! Just like the time Skip finally convinced me to take it and find out just how great it can feel! Come on man — flip over and give me that ass! We need to do this and get back inside watching the game, before the gals come home. Flip man — flip over! Give me that ass!"

Chapter Four: Go Slow — Please Go Slow!

"Jim flip over here and get your butt up in the air! I'm gonna run inside and grab some hand cream to use as a lube. That is one thing that Skip did teach me, yeah gotta have some lube back there! I'll be right back!"

Bob took off for the house and very slowly, with some hesitation, yet with some anxiety and some slight rush, Jim did flip over and present his "butt to the world." Anxious, yet timid, wanting it, yet still afraid of it, Jim knew the time had finally come that he was gonna get it in the ass, or he needed to refuse it, and realize that he would never again, have this opportunity. And an opportunity that included a dick big enough to make him realize that if he could successfully take Bob's rod, then any others that he might decide to take in the future, definitely were going to fit.

Bob came back out onto the patio, with the hand cream that he had run in to get. As he squeezed a small amount of cream onto Jim's ass, he told him, "Hey man, I'm gonna give your ass some cream and slide some up inside with my fingers, so don't get all nervous when you feel something going up in there, it's just a finger, OK?"

Taking a deep breath and still trying to relax, now with his buddy, Bob, straddling his legs and positioned right up on top of his butt, Jim finally managed to mutter an, "OK. But Bob, please, please go slow! Please man, I know you tell me this is gonna be good, but I am still fucking nervous about you putting that damn big dick of yours up in my ass. Now seriously man, if I find out I can't take it, you'll stop, right?"

"Yeah, I will man, I will! I can answer that question quite easily since I know damn sure that once you feel me up in there, you sure as the hell ain't gonna ask me to pull it back out. Seriously Jim, that's the honest truth! Once I'm up in there, you're gonna be bitching and groaning about not doing this earlier! Lay still and let me do it! It ain't gonna hurt, well—maybe just a real little when I first punch in, but seriously man, that will only be for a second and then you're gonna be begging for more dick!"

Bob rubbed Jim's butt hole, inside and out with some of the hand cream, and slid first one finger, then an additional finger, up into Jim's butt hole to start getting it opened up some.

"See there! That's feeling pretty good isn't it man?" Bob asked as he roamed around inside of Jim's butt for a few minutes.

"Yeah, yeah it feels good, but your fingers sure aren't the same as that damn stick you've got back there man! Your fingers are a hell of a lot smaller than that damn dick of yours! Seriously Bob, maybe you don't realize just how fucking big that damn thing is! I sure didn't know you were packing that much until tonight! Shocked the hell out of me when I finally saw it, and hard no less!"

"Hey man, it ain't that big! Seriously man, it might be a little bigger than normal, but I'm sure it's not that fucking big. Hell, my doctor has seen it and he's never said anything about it being way too big. Hey, if it was that out of normal, don't you think Skip would have said something about it? He never did! I know damn well it's been looked at in a lot of restrooms when I was taking a piss, and nobody ever acted shocked with it. Let's face it man, just cause it's gonna go up in your ole shit chute, you've got this idea it's a hell of a lot bigger than it really is. Hey, Cole sure didn't act freaked out over it, did he?"

"Well no, I guess you're right. Cole took it, and he never made any weird comments about it, so I guess maybe you're right, I'm just nervous as hell cause I know you're gonna push it up inside of me! OK man, I'll shut the hell up and trust you! But Bob, please! Like I asked, please go slow!"

With a laugh in his voice, Bob added, "I'm going slow man, real slow! Fact is, I'm going so damn slow, I may never get it up in there!"

"OK, OK! I'm sorry!" Jim rather pleaded. "Do me, just do me. Put it in me, I'll shut the hell up!"

Slowly and with care, Bob directed his rod meat directly at Jim's hole and realizing that the tip of his dick was correctly lined up, Bob leaned forward and started the penetration.

"Oh shit man, oh shit, you're starting in, aren't you? I can feel it! Oh Bob, go slow, please, go slow!"

"Like I already told you man, if I go any slower, I'm never going in!"

"OK, OK! I'll shut up! It's started in though isn't it? You've got the head of your dick in me, don't you?"

"Yeah, yeah! But just the head. Lay still and relax man, relax! Seriously Jim, in about 30 seconds, once I feed you the rest of this, you're gonna be begging for more! We've got your little butt hole opened, my dick's inside, now all I need to do is feed you the rest of it. Lay still, relax, and let me fuck you, OK?"

"OK — OK — OK!" Jim did manage to reply. I'm trying man, seriously, I'm trying!"

"OK you're doing OK, just lay there and let me go in!"

Finally, Jim did! He finally shut up and finally let Bob start poking his dick up into his butt.

"Hey man, I'm going in, I'm going in! How you feeling? You OK?"

"Yeah, I'm OK Bob, I'm OK! Yeah, I can feel it going up in me! Yeah — that's OK! Push just a little more! I can feel the head of your dick up in me! Yeah, push a little more."

"Lay still, lay still — you've got me! I'm in! You've taken my whole dick! You OK?"

"No — you're not all the way in me yet, are you? No Bob, don't shit around with me! You don't have all of it up in me, do you? You can't have!

No man, put the rest in me, but go slow!"

"Jim, you've got it! It's in you — all of it's in you! Here lay still! Let me push on your butt with my gut so you can tell, I'm not lying — you have all of it!"

Bob pushed and poked on Jim's butt a couple of times to let Jim have the feeling of his body attempting to push more and more up inside of him, if there was any more to push in.

"Oh shit man, you're not kidding. I really have your whole dick up in me, don't I? God Bob, I can't believe this! Push on me, push! Shit man, you're right, damn man, that feels good! Oh shit man, Bob, I'm not kidding, that I thought for sure, that once that damn thing went up in me, that I was really gonna feel it poking my guts up in there! Bob, you're right! Damn man, that feels good! Oh man, I'm sorry I was such a whiner! Oh shit Bob, I'm sorry! Seriously man, I thought it was really gonna hurt! It don't hurt at all! Hey, push on me some more, let me feel you pushing on my butt!"

Bob, did! He had just been given, in his mind anyway, the 'OK' to fuck him! And he did! He was finally in Jim's asshole, he was in all the way, Jim was liking it, and he was now asking for some action back there. Bob, started using Jim's butt like it had been used that way a lot!

"Jim, —baby, —honey, —you is getting fucked! You is getting fucked!"

"Oh my God Bob, I can't believe this! Yeah man, yeah! Do that! Yeah, slam me man, slam me! Oh Bob, I am so sorry I was such a crybaby! I am! God Bob, you are right! You kept trying to tell me I'd beg for more, yeah — God man — you were right! Shit man, pound me, pound my ass! Oh God man, I never thought getting fucked in the ass could feel like this! Oh shit man! Oh Bob, I probably shouldn't say this, but fuck man, now I'm wishing that Al guy, when I saw that big boner on him, oh shit I wish he'd have fucked me back then! Oh shit man, imagine that guy doing me with that fucker he had! Oh God, I'll bet his buddy loved getting it. Oh Bob, I had no idea getting it up the ass would feel anything like this! Oh shit man, now I understand why you wanted me to fuck you! Oh shit man! God, I wonder if Cole likes to fuck or just suck! Oh God man, I hope he's got a big dick!"

Bob was quite astounded at how vocal Jim had gotten all of a sudden — once he had, 'ass-eaten,' all of Bob's dick and actually had found out that it was fun — it did feel good, and —it did not hurt at all. Jim's comments about how he now wishes that he had been fucked by Al, back when he was a paperboy, rather excited Bob, but at the same time, created this uncomfortable feeling. He admitted to himself that he was personally glad it had never happened. He was secretly wishing, though, that Al, the man with the unbelievably big dick, was there, right then, so that he could see just how big that dick was, and if it was big, and maybe bigger than normal, get the chance to feel it up inside of his own butt hole! Just that possible idea, made his own butt hole twitch with excitement and hunger!

"Oh shit man, I am so damn embarrassed at the way I acted! Oh Bob, I like this! Pound me man, pound me!"

"I am man, I am. Seriously man, I can't keep this up much longer, I'm getting way too close to cumming man — I'm getting close!"

"Good, good! I wanna feel it explode inside of my ass! I want to know what it feels like up in there! Shoot off in me man, shoot off! Let me feel it Bob, let me feel it!"

"Oh shit man — oh shit! Hang on Jim — it's coming — it's coming! Hang on man — I'mmmm cumming! I'mmmmm cumming! Oh God Jim! Oh shit man, your ass has got to be loaded! Oh shit man, what a fucking cum that was. Oh God man, I'm whipped, man, I'm whipped. Hey, can I lay here on you for a minute or two? Oh shit man, I gotta recoup here some! Man, I am wiped out!"

"Yeah man. Lay there! Oh yeah, I love feeling you laying on top of me and your dick up in me! Oh Bob, damn man, I wish we'd been doing this all the time. Shit man, for as many hard-ons as we both have had while screwing around, trying to feel each other up in the pool, shit man, we could have been doing this! Damn man, I like this!"

After Bob laid there for a couple of minutes, he finished pulling out of Jim's butt, and reminded Jim that just perhaps they needed to get tided up a little and then get back into the house and get the game on and eat some of the pizza, just to make things look a little normal, before the wives came home.

"Bob, all I can say right now is, 'Thanks!' If you had not had the guts to tell me to drop the towel and turn around and face you, this would've never happened! I told you I've been curious about gay sex ever since seeing that Al guy, and now I finally know it is heaven, true heaven! Damn man, I can not believe that getting a dick, like that one of yours, pounded in and out of my ass, can feel so fucking good! Thank God that Skip guy fucked you that first time so that you knew what in the hell it was like. I'm sorry I was such a fucking baby about it! Really, I just knew it had to hurt like hell to have something like that stuck up in there! Boy — was I wrong!"

"Jim, I have looked at that ass of yours ever since the first time we were in the pool together, and all I can say right now, is I wish to hell I had fucked it a long time ago. Thank God we ordered pizza tonight! Shit man, I can not believe that Cole is gonna let us use his place anytime we want!"

"Bob, Thursday is too damn far away for me! I think maybe we each need to maybe, "go to the office" or do something else for a little while tomorrow, oh say, about maybe one o'clock or so, and go use Cole's place. Seriously man, I need fucked again! I'm serious! I know I just got it, but Bob — I need to get it again!"

Bob looked at Jim and with a big grin on his face, he nodded and agreed. "I agree, I definitely do! If we do, I sure as hell hope that Cole can be there too. I've never done it before, but I want to try fucking your ass at the same time that Cole is pounding mine!"

"Oh shit man, wow! Shit man, that sounds hot as hell to me! Course that means then, that after you fuck me and get fucked by Cole at the same time, then I want us to switch so that I can do the same thing. You think maybe we ought to try and call Cole to see if we can come over tomorrow? He told us his phone number is a cell number, and we can call any time. What'd you think?"

Bob looked at Jim, and said, "Come on man, let's get inside so that nothing looks funny, and then I'll call Cole and check with him. OK?"

Jim agreed, and both men grabbed a towel and tidied themselves up some, put their trunks back on, and headed back inside. After getting somewhat re-organized, Bob did call Cole.

"Hey Cole, this is Bob, you know from earlier tonight. Can you talk for a minute? Good! Hey guy, Jim finally got it up in the butt tonight, and after we got done, he decided that next Thursday is too far away. We were talking, and since tomorrow is a Saturday, we thought that maybe we could each come up with something that we each need to go do at about maybe one o'clock, and maybe, if it's OK with you, come visit your place for a little while. And, if it's possible for you to be there, we've talked about the idea of getting fucked while fucking another guy, so we're kind of hoping you can be there too. Can you be there? Would that be OK with you?"

After being silent for a moment, then Bob stated, 'No, but I sure don't have anything against it!' and then almost yelled into the phone, "Oh my God man — oh shit that would be great! Oh, I can't believe this! Yeah, yeah man — yeah, we'll see you tomorrow at right about one! Thank you man, thank you! Cole, we'll see you tomorrow! Bye!"

Jim was standing there in complete interest since Bob had gotten so excited during the conversation, and just as soon as Bob hung up, Jim asked, "What? What in the hell did he say? What's up?"

"He wants us there! He said, "Hell yes! He told me that the hottest one of his state trouper guys is stopping by right after he gets off of duty at noon tomorrow and he wants us to meet him. He told me he is one fucking hot guy, and loves to play and play good! He said that guy has got the dick of death on him, about ten inches or more when it's hard, and muscles to die for! He asked me if I'd ever played with a black man before, and I told him, 'No, but I sure don't have anything against it!' He said that trouper is a big built, muscled, black man, that loves to fuck and fuck hard! Oh my God man! I don't know if I can keep myself calm and collected until then! Oh shit man, this is unbelievable! Hey Jim, you don't have anything against playing with a black man do you? Especially — one with muscles and a ten inch rod on him?"

"Bob, Al was a black man! I didn't tell you that, cause I wasn't sure how you'd take that! I was afraid that if I told you that, then you'd think I was just making it up or something! This is gonna make all my dreams come true! Well, anyway, it sure as hell will come as close to being actually fucked by Al, as I'm sure I'll ever get! My God, I've got a ragging hard-on that really hurts! Oh God man, I'm so glad you fucked my ass today! Oh man, I'm so glad I've been fucked! Shit man, what a day! What a day!"

"Yeah, and tomorrow is gonna be even better! I know damn well it is! Jim, for a guy that just a little while ago, you weren't sure you even wanted my dick up in there, you sure are anxious to get that big, thick, ten incher up in there now, aren't you? God, you're horny for it aren't you man?"

"Yeah man, yeah! Seriously, my days of just dreaming about what Al could have done to me, has just about come to an end. After tomorrow, I'll have the real thing to remember! Well it might not be Al's, but it sure will be close enough that maybe I'll be able to think I finally got it from him. I know I'm really telling you my big secret now, but Bob, I've always wished that Al would have fucked my asshole with that big pole of his. Tomorrow, I'm gonna get him to fuck me and I'm just gonna close my eyes and make believe I'm still passing papers and that's Al in my butt! Oh man, oh shit, I never thought this could happen! I know I was just a teenaged kid then, but after I saw it standing up there so big and straight, I've wanted it in me, ever since! Every time I went to their house after that, I prayed I'd get to see it again, but it never happened. One day, I almost asked him if I could see it again, but then I chickened out! I knew his buddy wasn't home that day, and I really, really wanted to just tell him I wanted to see it and touch it! Oh Bob, I'm serious, I've dreamt of touching that cock ever since! I've dreamed and dreamed about what it would have been like to either get it stuffed up in me, or at least get to grab hold of it. Bob, I'm telling you everything else — I might as well tell you that on our wedding night, I laid there in bed having sex with my new bride, and I was wondering — while I was fucking her — what it would be like to have sex with Al! I actually was fucking her, and wishing at the same time that I was getting fucked by that great big mahogany dick! I know I was a cry baby tonight about taking your dick up in my ass, and that's really the way I was feeling about it, I was scared, but you know man — I have always known, that if it ever happened that Al was gonna fuck my butt, I know I would have just plain laid down and told him to go for it! I have always been that hot for that great big dark stick of dick! If I could have gotten fucked by him, I would have begged for it and never cared if it was tearing me up or not! I've wanted that dick in me for years now, and if I could have gotten it, I would have let him do it to me, without saying one word about him or his dick hurting my ass! Crazy, I know! I know thinking that way is crazy, but honestly man, the sight of that dick, and even remembering it sticking up that way — this many years later, it has always made me weak. Oh, I wanted to go in that room that morning, pull my pants down and just sit down on that dick! Oh, how I have re-lived that dream so many, many, times. Just the idea of walking in, straddle him laying there on the floor, grabbing my ass and pulling it open far enough to just sit down on that big pole and make it go all the way up inside of me! Oh, I've stuck some funny stuff up in my asshole just trying to make believe I've got his big thick dick stuck up in me! I had never, ever, thought about putting stuff up in my butt, until that day, and that dick! When I saw that dick, that was the first time I ever thought about what it would feel like to put something up in my butt! Bob, I had never thought about fucking asses or putting something up in your ass before. Automatically that morning, I just knew, all of a sudden, that it had to feel good, to get something like that big dick stuck up in your asshole! Oh Bob, this is way too much to believe! You, me, Cole, and now a hot black state trooper that looks like Al did! This is hot, man, fucking hot! Oh man, I hope he looks just like Al did! Oh man, I want him to fuck the hell out of me! God, I hope I can sleep tonight. Right now I feel like some little five year old kid, and tomorrow is Christmas!"

Chapter Five: But I Just Had To Do It!

"Hey guys, come on in!" Cole yelled as he realized that Bob and Jim had just arrived and had knocked on the front door.

Bob had used the excuse that he needed to go into the office to get some important paper work done, and Jim had used the excuse that he wanted to do some running around to see what kind of a used truck he could possibly find. Not wanting it to look obvious that the two neighbors had "left" at the same time, and later had "come home" at the same time, they had each used their own cars, and had agreed that they would not return at the same time, but that one would get home slightly earlier than the other.

As Bob and Jim entered the apartment, Cole looked up at them, from his position of laying on the living room floor, gut down, butt in the air, and one damn hot looking muscular black man pounding on his ass.

In between body slams and quick attempts of catching his breath, Cole managed a, "Hey guys give me just a second or two and I'll be right with you. Give me a sec and I'll introduce you to Jason. Give us just a sec, I think he's about to unload in me, and I sure don't want to miss that!"

As Jason was pounding the hell out of Cole's ass, he looked up at Bob and Jim and nodded a pleasant, "Hello."

"Hey guys, get yourselves comfortable while Jason finishes up here on me. OK?"

Just as Bob and Jim each started to say, "OK", Jason let out a major groan and softly said, "Hang on man, this cops gonna explode! Here I come man, here I cum! Oh Cole I love your ass man — I love your ass — eat my cum man — oh shit man — eat my cum!"

As Bob and Jim did start to get undressed, they obviously were strongly drawn to the actions that were in the process of happening in the middle of the living room floor! Jason, the hot black cop, was obviously in the process of planting a lot of seed in Cole's little white asshole.

"Oh pound me, pound me, pound me man," was about all Cole could get out of his mouth for the entire time that Jason was feeding his ass with what had to be major, major, future, muscle growing, semen.

Slowly Cole managed to turn his head toward Bob and Jim, and while Jason was still laying on top of him, and still in him, Cole said, "Hey guys, I got him all warmed up for you. He's in the mood, and he's wanting some new ass."

Jason looked up at the two men, and simply grinned.

Bob and Jim had succeeded in getting all undressed, but feeling rather uncomfortable in just what they were expected to do, when suddenly Jason said, "Hey Hon, hold on, I'm pulling out!"

As Cole laid there with his arms spread out wide, in a complete comfortable position, he felt Jason raise up some, and all of a sudden his ass felt terribly empty! "Oh shit man, you're out! Damn it man, I always feel so all alone after you pull out!"

Starting to get up from the position on the floor and of course on top of Cole, as well as in Cole, Jason laughed and replied, "Well man, all I can say is buy yourself a big butt plug and make believe that's me in you when you've got that stuck up in there!"

Jason, of course, managed to get up from the floor before Cole did, and he greeted both Bob and Jim by extending his hand out and telling them, "Hi guys, I'm Jason. Been anxious to meet both of you! Cole told me about yesterday, out by the pool, and I told him I want to help teach both of you guys the good stuff that can be done with each other. OK?"

Bob and Jim each attempted an "OK" in reply but with both men being so overtaken with the sight that they were now seeing, made if hard to be very coherent. Jason looked to be about 34 or 35 years old, stood about six foot three, had a chest of probably 54 or 55 inches, a waist of only about 33 or 34 inches, a neck of about 18 inches, biceps of probably 18 or 19 inches, thighs of maybe 25 or 26 inches, calves of at least 20 inches and a dick of death of more than the reported ten inches. Both men actually stood there with their mouths hanging wide open and staring at the sight.

"Pretty damn impressive ain't it guys?' Cole asked, as he got up from the floor, walked up behind Jason, bent over to his butt and then ran his tongue up the entire length of Jason's back. "Hot man, ain't he guys?"

"Hey knock it off man, knock it off!" Jason asked of Cole. "Everybody has their own positive attributes, and I just happen to be a big guy! Everybody's got their main points, and hey Cole — yours is pizza, and a damn hot ass, I might add!" Jason laughed as he attempted to get Cole to quit making comments about his build.

"So I guess you guys ain't had a chance in that ass of Cole's yet right?"

Shaking his head "No," Bob replied. "No, sure haven't. We've got to admit that after he left yesterday, we even made a comment that we failed to see what kind of a dick he's got. Got to admit, yesterday was a pretty nervous situation for us. Gotta remember we have a couple of wives to worry about, and even though they weren't supposed to, we still had to be afraid that for some unknown reason, they could have come home, right at the wrong time. So yeah, gotta admit, we never got to really know Cole in the up close and real tight way!"

Jim silently stood there and continued to admire Jason, all of Jason, including his enormous rod, as he and Bob spoke, and Cole silently stood by. Suddenly, sounding almost in shock, Jim finally said, "Bob, he looks just like Al, he's bigger, but he looks just like Al, and that's what Al's dick looked like!"

With Jason and Cole completely in the dark about what in the world Jim was talking about, Bob then told Jason and Cole about the experience that Jim had, back in his newspaper days with his customer Al. During the conversation of explanation about Al, Jim did tell them about how he has always wished he could have just gone into that living room, dropped his pants and the just squatted down completely onto Al's stiff hard-on!

Looking over at Jim, reaching out and placing his mammoth hand on Jim's shoulder, Jason then said. "OK tell you what! Let's play that out! You put your pants back on, go back outside, look in through the screen door like you did that day years ago, then come on in and do whatever you have been wishing you could have done then! OK? Game?"

"Oh shit man, are you kidding? You kidding? That sounds so fucking hot to me! Really, you mean it?"

47

"Hell yeah I do! I'll be in here on the floor, and Cole and Bob can be doing something, whatever they feel like doing, and you just come in and do whatever it was, you wanted to do to that Al guy that day!"

Everybody agreed this was definitely a good start and all got into their respective positions. Jason had excused himself for just a moment to go to the bathroom as everybody else got rather ready. Jason explained that he wanted to rather tidy up some just in case Jim decided he wanted to start with some tongue action — and he did not want his dick tasting like ass juice, and maybe turning Jim off. Cole and Bob laid down on the floor, as if perhaps there had been three men in that living room that day instead of just the two, and Jason returned and laid down on his back, with a major hard-on sticking up in the air! Jim had gotten his pants back on, just incase somebody did happen to be out side in the courtyard area. He went outside, then turned and looked in through the screen door.

Much to Jim's surprise, this did actually feel very much like the original day. As he looked into the living room, he could see the massive black man, laying there on the floor, supporting a major hard-on. Jim's only difference this time was, he had actually seen this hard-on before, and his initial shock of seeing it for the first time did not of course happen again.

As Jim stood at the door, he admired the cock, and the entire body. He silently, as if sneaking in, opened the door, stepped inside, closed the door, and for a minute just stood there. He gazed at what he knew he was going to get to use to his complete fulfillment and enjoyment, in only a minute or so.

Silently Jim removed his pants. Knowing more now than he would have at the age of a teenager, he took advantage of the can of Crisco sitting on the corner of the blanket that was spread out on the floor. He applied a good amount onto his ass, and pushed another good amount, up inside. Silently he moved over toward Jason, stepped his right foot over him, straddled his body, and started to squat down.

Cole and Bob very silently laid on the floor, hugging each other as if asleep, although silently watching just what Jim was doing.

Jim steadied himself and continued to squat even more. He reached back behind himself and aimed the tip of Jason's long, thick, dick right at his asshole. Continuing to squat, and feeling the tip of the meat pole touching right at his rose bud, he actually threw his feet out from under himself and immediately, he sat down fully — he sat down completely — and he sat down hard! He let out an excruciating yell of pain, and Jason jumped and yelled, "Oh my God! Oh shit man, you OK?"

Cole and Bob both immediately flew up off of the floor and both immediately asked, "Jim, you OK?"

"Oh my God yes! Oh God yes, I'm OK! Oh God, oh lordy man, that fucking hurt! Oh shit man, I am so fucking full back there! Oh Jason, I've got all of your cock up in there! The whole damn thing! Oh, I've got your whole fucking damned dick up in me! Oh man, oh shit — that's what I wanted — that's what I wanted. I did it man — I did it!"

"Once again Jason asked, "Jim, you OK? You OK? Man, you actually impaled yourself on that dick! God man, I thought you'd go down on it slowly man, I did! I've never been able to slam it up in some guy's ass like that! No guy has even taken it like that! You OK?"

"Hey guys, I'm OK! I had to do that! Let me sit here for a minute and catch my breath! I'm OK."

"Jim, why in the hell did you slam down on that thing like that? Shit man, do you realize how fucking big his dick is? Jim, you out of your mind?"

Looking over at Bob, Jim replied, "Yeah I probably am man, I probably am, but that's what I dreamt about for the last 10 or 12 years. Hey man, he was giving me the chance to do what I have wished I had done a long time ago, and I needed to do it! Thank God you fucked me yesterday. I knew, kind of what getting it up the ass was like since you fucked me yesterday, and today, I just had to do it! I had to take all of it just as fast as I could! Oh Jason, thanks man! Thank you for letting me do this! I didn't hurt you when I did that, did I? I didn't, did I?"

"No Jim you didn't, but man it scared the hell out of me the way you just slammed down on it without so much as letting your ass get used to it! Shit man I was just hoping you were OK!"

"God I know it was probably stupid, but I just had to do it like I know I would have tried to do, back then. I know that Sunday morning when I was looking in at him and saw that pole standing up there so big and so tall, I know that I just kept wanting to sneak in there, and just sit down on it as fast as I could, so today, I just had to do it like that! I did it, stupid maybe, but I did it! Thank goodness for the can of Crisco sitting there though. I'm smart enough now, to know though, that without it, if I'd tried to do it without that grease, I'd still be screaming in major, major, major pain! Thank goodness for Crisco!"

"God almighty Jim!" Bob exclaimed. "Shit man! Yesterday you were so fucking afraid of me fucking you, and now here today, you take a fucking telephone pole without so much as a whimper! Man, I sure can see now, just how much you have been wishing you had fucked yourself on that Al's dick that day! Jim, are your insides OK? Jim, you sure you're OK?"

"Hey Bob, look at me! Look at me! Look at what I'm sitting on! Look at what in the hell I'm sitting on top of! Just imagine what is stuck up inside of me! Look at the hunk of beef under me! And you ask me if I'm OK? I'm in fucking heaven, fucking heaven right now! All I gotta do now is to see if I can get this hunk of a man that I'm sitting on, to maybe reach up here and pinch my tits! Oh man, I wanna feel his fingers on me! Please Jason, pinch me! Play with my nipples!"

Jason smiled, said, "Oh yeah man, yeah I will! The way you just used my dick on yourself, I'll do anything you ask! You want if rough and tight, I assume, right?"

Jim did not say anything. He simply looked directly into Jason's eyes, smiled a broad grin, and licked his lips. Jason knew he had himself a new playmate that was wanting it rougher and tougher than any of his other guys. Jason knew that the time had finally come for him to take advantage of his strength and bulk in letting some guy reach his ultimate goal of sexual excitement! He grabbed each tit and decided to see if Jim could take as much pain on his sweet little virgin tits, as he had just taken up in his ass! Jason knew he had a man sitting on him that was gonna be a willing partner to all types of actions that most gays shy away from. He knew, just intuitively knew, that with the way Jim had taken the initiative to impale himself without caution, onto his enormous 11 inch long and six and a quarter inch round meat rod, that he now had a man to be treated with respect and, admiration and to also be treated as any, rough and ready, fucker needs to be treated! Real rough and ready! Jason was hot with the idea that this man wanted, was rough enough to take it, and knew how in the hell to go and get it! He looked up at Jim and secretly smiled at him with ideas still locked in his head, that even Jim could not imagine.

Being completely in shock at the way Jim had suddenly and without any warning at all, had actually impaled himself onto Jason's enormous dick, Cole and Bob laid back down and attempted to get their attention onto something else. Cole laid down, and immediately reached over to Bob and grabbed onto his dick. "Come on man, let's get this thing hard again like last night! I need to eat me some more Bob meat. It tasted so good yesterday, I need more!"

Suddenly Bob looked directly at Cole and stated, "Hey wait a minute man. Talk about tasting so good — you never got paid last night for the pizza. We gotta pay you for the pizza today before we leave!"

Laughing, Cole looked at Bob and replied, "Shit man! I'm about ready to eat your dick, suck all the manhood out of it, and all you can think of is you didn't pay for the pizza last night? That's how excited you are that you are about to feed me your dick, that you worry about paying for pizza!?"

Realizing about how weird his comment might have sounded right then, Bob did laugh back about it, but then added, "Hey man! We were so fucking happy that you got involved in our goofing around, we didn't want you coming up on the loosing end. We don't want you paying for our pizza!"

"Hey believe me man, I did not come up on the loosing end — not by no means! I got me some meat in the action, some that I had been hoping for, for a long time! And I got both of 'em, not just one of 'em. Don't worry about the pizza! It got paid for! And I collected for it, understand? There's more than one way of getting paid! Money is not always the right way!"

Cole then immediately took all of Bob's rod down into his throat and sucked on it like it was gonna get away. Bob grabbed hold of the sides of Cole's head and jerked it back and forth, as if he was using it as a jerk off device on his dick. He let out an enthusiastic yell of, "Yeah man, yeah! Yeah that feels good, do it, do it!"

Bob and Cole were frantically in the actions of each man getting a major blow job from his companion, as Jim and Jason were letting Jim discover all of the comforts of having a very hot and active man, not only fucking his ass with what had often been referred to as "the dick of death," but also playing with his tits, as if neither man had ever realized they are only on a man for this type of sexual enjoyment.

A Jason and Jim were involved in the excitement of enjoying each other, Jason suddenly asked Jim to "Jump up and down! I wanna feel my dick sliding up and down inside of you! Yeah man, yeah! Yeah can you feel that? Oh man that makes my dick feel so good! Hey man, keep that up, it's about to make me cum! I'm gonna cum, keep that up! Keep it up, keep it up! Oh shit man that makes my dick feel so good, keep it up! Keep it up! Oh shit man, get ready to feel some hot cum hitting you — keep jumping on it! Oh man — here it comes — here it comes! Oh my God, that feels so good loading you up in there like that! Shit man, it's been a long time since I've cum up in some guy while I was laying on my back and he was jumping up and down on my cock! Oh man — oh shit, what a great feeling! Oh man, can you feel that, can you feel that?"

"Oh shit yes man, shit yes I can feel that! Damn man, did your dick get bigger and harder since I sat down on it? Damn man, it really does feel like a railroad car up in there now! Shit man, my ass feels really spread! Fucking full and really spread wide open!"

Then looking over at Bob, Jim asked, "Hey guy, you gonna get fucked with this pole? Last night you were the one that was ready to go climb the utility pole and make believe you had this stud on top of you, you gonna take it?"

Looking over toward Jim, Bob pulled off of Cole's dick for just a moment and stated, "Yeah, as long as you don't wear it out first! I want him to fuck me while I fuck one of you guys, OK?"

Hearing that, Cole then pulled off of Bob's dick and told the guys, "Hey guys. I need to leave in just a few minutes. I need to be at the pizza shop by two, so why don't you guys hold off on that until after I have to be gone, cause I want to play with Jim some and let him suck on me if he will, before I have to go! Is that OK with you guys?"

Both Bob and Jim responded with a "Yeah" and Bob then asked Cole if he wanted to switch and take Jim for a few minutes before he had to leave.

Cole said, "Yeah, if that's OK with him."

Looking over at Cole, Jim replied, "Yeah that's OK with me! I'm in for anything and everything!"

Jason obviously heard the plan of actions and he looked up at Jim, smiled and then said, "Pull that ass up and off, but don't let it get too closed, I want some more of it, yet. But I think it's time now to see just how fast Bob can take it! You game Bob?"

"Yeah, yeah man! Yeah I want it, and I will admit I want it badly, but don't expect me to go slamming down on it like Jim did! I'm gonna need to take some time getting it up in me, OK?"

"Hell yeah that's OK!" Jason stated. "Gotta admit Jim was the first and only guy that ever went onto it like he did. Shocked the hell out of me! And I'm still surprised that he managed to do it. Hey Bob, I'm very used to letting some guy's ass get used to it before I go all the way in. Trust me man, you'll do OK on it!"

As Jim got his feet back under himself, he started to stand up and let the enormous, yet delicious massive dick start to slide back out of his ass. "Oh shit man, oh shit! Oh man that feels so fucking good sliding back out! Oh shit man I gotta admit it hurt like fucking hell when I slammed down on it, but shit man, I can sure feel all of it up in there now! Oh Jason, oh yeah man, yeah I want that back up in me later! Hey, fuck my buddy Bob, but be careful, he's got a fragile ass!"

"Hey let me show the man it's not fragile. He just may need to go in me a lot slower than you took him, but I think he'll still have fun!"

Jason got up from on the floor, assuming that Bob wanted to be laying on the floor and letting Jason poke into him from above.

Cole took Jim by the dick and said, "Yeah man, yeah! I want this! I tasted this one last night and I want it again! Come here man, feed me that dick of yours!"

Jim moved up close to Cole's mouth, and stuck it in! "Here man, suck me again, yeah suck me like you did last night!"

Cole was seated on the floor and Jim was standing in front of him, feeding him his slick stick of meat! "Eat me man, eat me! Get that damn thing good and real stiff, cause I wanna stick it up your ass before you have to get out of here. Suck me big time, big time!"

"You about ready Bob? You get all greased us?"

"Yeah I'm greased, but I still do need to ask you to take it good and slow back there! I want it, and I want it bad, but my ass just might not take it as fast as Jim's did. I still think he was out of his fucking mind for slamming down on it as fast as he did! I'm just fucking glad we don't have to rush him to a hospital! Damn man, I'm sure I wouldn't have had the nerve to poke something that fucking big up in my ass like that! I'm just glad he's OK!"

"Yeah, I gotta agree, I'm glad he's OK too! I suppose a guy could get some damage done by taking it up in his ass that fast, but thank goodness it's never happened. Now, I'm gonna go in you a lot slower than that, you ready?"

"Oh yeah man, yeah I'm ready!" Bob anxiously answered to the massive hunk of man that was now ready to start his enormous entry into his ass.

Bob laid there on the floor with his arms spread out, and his legs spread enough to let Jason position right on top of him, and be able to gain entry. "Just go slow, please, go slow! Oh yeah-yeah-oh Jason, I can feel it already!"

Jason realized that pushing his rod up into an ass that was not quite opened for it yet, could and usually does, create some very uncomfortable feelings for his bottom man, so he was taking it very slowly.

"Yeah push man, push! Oh shit man, I can feel that! It feels good, but yeah I can feel it! Oh Jason just knowing that I'm getting that big thing of yours up in my ass is exciting and makes me really horny, but got to admit, thinking about all of that up inside of me really makes me nervous!"

"Well man, you just lay there and let me take care of you, you are doing good! Doing real good!"

Jason wrapped his hands around to the chest of Bob and squeezed it as he pushed more of his black man steel rod up into Bob's ass. Slowly but steadily, he continued to push, but yet at the same time hugged Bob's chest, to maybe kind of keep Bob's mind onto something else other than how full his ass was getting and how far opened it was being spread! Push, by push, Jason was making his way!

"Oh man, that feels so good! How much you got in me? How far are you?"

"I'm in man — I'm in! You've got it all! I've got all of it up in you! You've got it! You OK?"

"Oh my God man, do you!? Do you really have that whole fucking thing up in me!?"

"Yeah, I do! I won't lie to you man, you have it!"

"Oh God then fuck me man, fuck me! Oh Jason I can't believe that feels that fucking good up in there! Please fuck me hard man, I wanna feel you fucking me hard!"

"Hang on man, hang on!" Jason suggested! "I've already cum twice today, once in Cole's butt and once in Jim's butt, but God oh live man, your ass is so fucking tight, it is getting me all loaded up again! I'm gonna pound you until I let it fly and can't stop it! Get ready man, I'm gonna fuck the hell out of you till I fall apart all over the top of you! Bob, hope your ass can take it, cause man, I'm going for it, and I'm going for it big time!"

"Do it, do it, do it!" Bob begged. "Come on man, I can take it, I can take it!"

Without further word, Jason started using Bob and his ass like it was some kind of a native wild animal out in the woods that only gets it once a year! With all of Jason's weight and size on top of him, Bob certainly could tell he was being pounded wildly and madly by one man that knew how to use his enormous dick!

It took a full five minutes of non-stop massive pounding, but all of a sudden Jason yelled out, "Oh shit man, hang on man, I'm cummmmmin man, oh shit — I'm cummmmmin! Oh God, I just came! Oh man, oh shit, oh crap man, I am fucking exhausted! Oh man, you OK? Oh shit man, I think I just hit you with more juice that I dumped in Cole and Jim combined! Damn man, I sure am glad I never plan on having anymore kids, cause I think I just finished giving you all the cum I can ever make. Man, your ass has got to be fucking full of cum! Wow, thanks man, thanks!"

"Hey, I don't know what in the hell you are thanking me for! I'm the one that got the fucking, let me thank you! Thanks man, —thanks!"

"Hey Bob, I guess maybe you don't realize that if I get that rough on most guys, they bitch and complain. Shit, even my cop buddies! Shit man, you just kept taking and taking, regardless of how rough I got back here! And part of the time, I was really pounding you harder and harder just to see if you'd beg me to stop! And you never did! You just kept acting like you were wanting more and more! Thanks! Besides, cause of you and Jim, this is really turning out to be a great day! I don't know if it's because both of you are really kind of new to this type of sex play or not, but my God man, both of you guys can really do it, and you do it the way I like it! Cole's good, he's fucking good, that's why I come over here and play with him, but shit man, the rest of my buddies are fucking wimps! If it's OK with you guys, I wanta make it a regular to get together with you guys. God, if Cole's not available, I sure as hell hope, one of you two will be! Damn man, you guys are good!"

During Jason's fucking marathon on top of Bob's butt, Cole had turned around and let Jim fuck his ass. That little session didn't last too long, cause Cole then told Jim that he really did need to go shower and get ready to get over to the pizza shop by two.

Jim understood, and just before he released Cole from his grip, he pounded into Cole about three more times, and then said, "This will continue! I've heard now from Jason over there about how you are really one of the best guys to play with, so count on me being back over here to get in on the good stuff!"

As Cole pulled his butt off of Jim's swollen rod, he looked back and replied, "You better damn well be! We're already set up for Thursday night, and we're gonna make hay man, we're gonna make hay!"

As Cole started to head for the bathroom to shower down and get ready to head for the pizza shop, he told the other three that he wanted them to stay as long as they wanted, especially since he knew both Bob and Jim were anxious to get fucked in the ass, while they fucked some other ass. Jason agreed that he definitely wanted to be part of that, either doing some fucking on the top, or letting one of the guys fuck his ass, whichever way worked out for them. He looked at the two and said, "Suppose you guys already know, I sure don't get fucked in the ass very often since everybody wants my dick up in their asses, so if either one of you so desire, it's there for the taking."

Both Bob and Jim grinned widely and replied, "OK man, OK! I hear you!"

Then Bob looked at Jim, shook his head and made a facial expression such as, "Wow man, I can't believe this!"

Jim returned the look, and then they, both, looked at Jason with a very wide assed grin on their faces and Jim said, "You are making our day man, you sure as the hell are!"

Jason grinned back, and said, "Good men, good! I sure am glad, since you two are making my day too! Come on, let's all go take a quick shower and kind of freshen up some, so that we can get back in here and start all over again. We got some serious three way fucking to do! And seriously men, I do hope one of you two will fuck my ass for me! I need it!"

Chapter Six: But for Me —!

Cole had taken a very quick shower and gotten dressed in his pizza uniform, which incidentally definitely did not show any of Cole's very positive body elements, which did include his own personally built pizza sausage that he did so proudly possess. He headed out the door to go deliver some pizzas, and in his mind — keep his eyes open for some more anxious hungry dick, that needed to be trained, in the sport of — "letting the pizza guy at it!"

As he left, Jason and the two hunky neighbors attempted to all fit into the tub to shower down and freshen up. Cole's apartment did not have a free standing shower, it was a shower in the tub, and now a tub that also had three hunky guys in it all at once.

Rather laughing, Bob stated, "You know something Jason? This is gonna be the first time Jim and I have been in a shower together. Seriously man, everything is happening so fucking fast! Hell man, 24 hours ago, neither one of us had even seen the other guys' dick, let alone putting it in our mouths or taking it up in our asses. Shit man, things sure have changed for us since about five o'clock yesterday!"

As he took the shower hose off of its perch and was spraying all three of the men down, Jason stated, "You gotta be kidding, right? Cole told me about the little session out by the pool yesterday, but I sure did not understand that was the first time you two did anything together! I thought he just meant it was the first time he had been involved with you guys."

"Oh no!" Jim entered. "No, that was really the first time for us. Bob's played around some before, but for me, that was really my very first time doing anything with a guy! The closest I had ever been to gay sex before was that day I stood there in the doorway and looked at that Al guy!"

Without saying anything, Bob took the shower head from Jason, and sprayed Jason down completely, from head to toe, and up under the crotch too. Moving his dick and his bag out of the way, Bob shot the warm water right at Jason's crotch and used his free hand to massage around under there to let Jason know he liked what he could see and feel! Jason stood there as he felt Bob's hand slide around and slide, ever so slightly, up into his ass crack, and felt a finger tip slide ever so slightly also, up and into his tight, muscle controlled, hole.

Handing the shower head to Jim, Bob managed to stoop down far enough to get his head under Jason's bag and suck his left nut into his mouth. His right hand was holding onto the base of Jason's cock, and his left hand was exploring Jason's massive muscle structure called, his ass.

"Oh my God man, yeah! Oh shit man, that feels so fucking good!"

Hearing Jason exclaim his pleasures of having one nut sucked, Bob then maneuvered so slightly so that he could suck Jason's right nut in beside the other.

The spacing in the tub was of course, very crowded, and all three men were by necessity, rather all lined up in a single row. Bob was in the middle, and of course stooped down so that he could suck in the soft brown bag of nuts that Jason could so proudly display. Jim was behind Bob, and by spreading his legs some, he managed to straddle Bob and lean forward enough to grab Jason around the lats, placing his thumbs right up and into his arm pits, and placing his mouth on Jason's massive muscular chest, so that he could suck in Jason's left tit! Jason slightly pushed his chest forward indicting that he did want his tits sucked and chewed on!

"Oh my God men, oh shit! Oh God, men this is great! This is great! Oh guys I haven't been treated this way for a hell of a long time. Oh men, oh shit! Oh God men, I love this! Oh guys, you guys are a great pair! Oh you guys really know how to take care of a guy! Oh men, do me, yeah, do me!"

Jason's expression of appreciation and his statements of how great this was feeling, definitely got Jim and Bob both, horny as hell and made both of them go after Jason's body with vim and vigor! Bob rolled Jason's balls around in his mouth as much as he possibly could. Bob's only fear was that due to the size of Jason's balls, he may not be able to keep both of them crammed in his mouth together. He did not want one to slide out, he wanted to keep sliding them back and forth, rubbing past each other, so that Jason could get a great ball rubbing, and bag sucking, experience.

Jim was grabbing Jason's lats on each side and that feeling, all by itself, was giving Jim a major hard-on that, due to his leaning over the top of Bob, was slapping Bob every time his dick moved. With each hand firmly placed on one of Jason's lats, and his fingers and thumbs, managing to massage Jason's armpits, Jim changed back and forth from sucking and chewing on Jason's left nipple, over to his right nipple, then back again!"

"Oh my God men, I can't believe this! Guys, I'm gonna cum! Seriously men, I'm gonna cum! I can't believe it, I'm not even touchin' my dick and I know I'm gonna cum!"

Managing as well as he could with two enormous male nuts stuck in his mouth, Bob did manage to utter, "Do it, do it! Cum, man cum!"

Hearing Jason's statement and excitement of getting ready to cum, and not even touching his dick, simply made Jim go outrageously horny and simply out of control, that he bit Jason's tits as hard as he could, to which Jason made no complaint, and as he bit, he then reach down with his left hand and grabbed onto Jason's dick.

"Oh my, oh my God!" Jason actually yelled, although in somewhat of a muffled way. "Oh men, oh men, oh men! Oh, I'm gonna cum, I'm gonna cum!"

Once again Bob managed a, "Yeah, do it man, do it!"

Suddenly Jason threw his head up, grabbed hold of the top of the shower door assembly, grabbed hold of the window crank on the other side of the tub, thrust his body forward and let it all fly!

"Oh men, oh men! Oh God men, I'm cumin, I'm cummmmin, I'm cummmin! Oh my God men, I just came again! I can't believe this, I just came again!"

Jim pulled back far enough to look down and watch Jason's cum, come flying out of the end of his enormous dick, and watch part of it land on Bob's chest and part of it hit his own legs.

Knowing what was happening as Jason's cum flew loose, Bob sucked hard, very hard, on Jason's nuts to give them the ultimate of sensations as the climax happened! He knew that even if he happened to be sucking or biting a little too hard, there was no way that Jason would ask for him to let up on them. He simply knew that cumming at the same time that your nuts feel like they are in a vice grip, had to be the ultimate feeling in having your nut bag sucked on, just as your cum is cutting loose, to fly as far a possible!

After giving Jason a minute or two, to either re-compose, or perhaps live in the life of luxury in being treated so royally, Bob finally let first one, brazil nut sized nut, pop out, and then the other. He licked the underside of Jason's bag before he managed to slide out from under Jason's crotch, and also out from under Jim. All three men, now stood there, once again in a man-beside-man straight line, and grinned widely at each other.

Jason was in heaven, and he knew it. He told the men that it had been a hell of a long time since two men, had taken him at the same time, and used him like that to such a total, total excitement!

Bob had just experienced the most exciting time of sucking on the biggest set of balls that he had ever felt, and actually the first set of balls that he had ever sucked into his mouth, and then rolled them around in there. Jim had managed to feel Jason's structure and grab onto his lat muscles and get a great understanding and appreciation of just what some big, thick, strong, muscles like those lats, do feel like. Having that much muscle in his hands, and knowing that the man that owned those muscles was letting him feel them was unbelievable! He had never sucked on another man's tits before, and that action, in itself, was just one more new exciting act, that he was now discovering, in his new adventures into the gay actions! He licked his lips and silently said to himself, "Thanks Jason, thanks! I liked that! I've never sucked on some other guy's chest before, and I liked that!"

As Jim stood there letting the shower water fall over him, he looked at Jason's nipples and smiled! He looked down at Jason's dick and smiled. He then just looked at Jason as well as he could, since the spacing was quite tight with all three men in the one tub, and he just said, "Damn man, this is great! Wow oh shit! This is great!"

Looking at Jim, Bob asked. "What? What do you mean? What are you talking about?"

"I'm talking about all of this! All of this! Never before did I ever imagine me living any part of my life like this. Bob, look at yourself! You are a hunk! You look like some guy that spends all day in the gym working out! You've got a body on you that I know damn well all of the women in your office talk about when they go to lunch together, and probably some of the guys too — if they're open enough to admit when a guy is a real hunk! Then look at this marble statue of a god standing in here with us! Jason, I never really looked at black men much, except for remembering back to that Al guy, I really didn't have any reason to. They were just men! My god man — how that has changed! Every time I see dark skin, I'm gonna cum in my jeans just remember you and what I got to do earlier when I slammed my ass down on that baseball bat of yours! Guys, you two guys are hot! Damn hot, and I'm getting to do all this good stuff with both of you! Shit man, this is great! Come on men, —I'm getting all horny and ready to get in there and have one of you fuck my ass while I fuck an ass!"

And then looking at Bob, Jim continued. "Hey man, remember how this stud asked us earlier if we'd fuck his ass since he don't get it often enough? Think maybe we might be able to do that?"

"Shit yes man, hell yes! I don't think you saw it when I was sucking on his bag down there, but my hand was going up in that butt, and it is a good butt! All I could think of when I was up in there exploring around was how I wanted to get my dick up in there! Jim, that is one hot ass! One hot ass! Come on men, let's get rinsed off and get back out there! We've got some serious man loving to do!"

All three men quickly rinsed off and each grabbed a towel and tried off!

With Jason happening to lead the way, all three men headed back toward the living room when Jim asked. "Hey Jason. You made a comment a little while ago about how you sure are glad you're not planning on having any more kids since you thought you'd used up all the cum, you could make. Did you used to be married? How many kids you got?"

Turning back to see Jim, Jason grinned and said, "Oh yeah, used to be, and still am! Got a boy and a girl! Jimmy's 12 and Sara's 13."

"Oh so you're still married, right?" Jim asked.

"Yeah, still the married guy!"

"So, I guess maybe then, the whole group of us are married guys, doing the fun stuff then, right?"

"Yeah, guess so. Cole told me you guys are married guys! I can understand your needing someplace to play. Trying to play at home when there's family there is kind of a bitch! Cole and I've played together for about two years now, so I really appreciate him letting me use his place whenever I need a hide out!"

As the three got to the living room and started laying back down on the floor, Bob then asked. "Well hey man, how long you been doing the guy thing? That something you started after you got married, or—uh, —like when did you start doing both sides of the fence?"

"Bout ten years ago! Yeah, just about ten years!"

"You had never played with guys before that?" Bob asked.

"No sure hadn't. Got kind of drunk one night, and without knowing it, I was being used by some guys, and kind of woke up in the middle of it!"

"What? What did you say!?" Jim almost exploded! "You did what!?"

"I got a promotion at the station where I was working out of, and some guys threw me a celebration party at one of the guys' houses. It was all drinking and drugging! I didn't do, and I never have done drugs, but I sure as hell over did my drinking that night! I guess maybe I was trying to keep up with my buddies by drinking ever time they hit something. I do know that some of them were pushing drinks at me all the time, telling me it was time for me to celebrate! Anyway, I finally passed out! It was later in the night, and most of the guys had left already, and only a small handful of us were still there! They were pouring some pretty strong stuff, and it went down smooth! Well anyway, I finally hit the floor and just went to sleep!"

Looking toward Jason with intense interest, Jim then said — "Yeah — you went to sleep! What in the hell happened then?"

"Well, I didn't know it until later, but I finally found out that some of the guys that set that party up, the same ones that were still there late, had an alterative motive in having that party."

"Yeah — what — hell I'm about afraid to ask — what alterative motive?" Bob asked.

"To see me naked! I've always been well built, most of it's natural, built just like my Dad, but anyway, those guys, from what I was later told, had tried many times to get me someplace where they could see me naked, and they finally decided to get me stoned drunk, let me pass out, and then undress me!"

"Oh shit man, shit!" Oh God Jason, is that what happened?"

"Yeah Bob, that is what happened! I don't know if either one of you guys have ever been so drunk that after you pass out, you might, for just a few seconds, kind of come to, but not enough to really control anything, but anyway, that's what happened to me that night! I passed out on the floor! They told me later that nobody knew I was out of it, they told me that I talked to them and answered questions just like I was all OK. Well, I must not have been, cause I found out later of a whole lot of stuff that happened that I really do not remember! There is one time, probably about 30 seconds worth of time that I remember, from sometime late in the middle of the night! Somebody had their hand kind of up in my butt, and I guess that kind of brought me too, but not enough to where I made him take it back out!"

As the three men laid there on the floor, Bob and Jim encouraged Jason to continue telling them of that night, that night he doesn't really remember! All three men had their hands everywhere, on everything each man could reach!

"Jason", Jim interrupted! "Keep talking man, this is making me horny as hell, so if I start fucking you or sucking you while you're telling us this, don't stop! Man, I'm about ready to fucking explode inside, so if I molest you while you are talking, don't let that interrupt you any! Come on man, I gotta hear this!"

"They told me, later, that they thought I had just laid down to rest, but they said I kept talking to them whenever I was asked something! They admitted later that they really did want me to just pass out, so they could strip me of my clothes, but they really thought I was still OK. They told me that's why they kept trying to give me more to drink. They wanted me laying there totally out of it!"

"Like what were they asking you? What did they want to know?" Bob inquired in intense interest!

I guess at first it was nothing important, things like did I want something else to drink, was I comfortable, did I feel a draft, stuff like that, until I guess it was Mikey that laid down beside me and started feeling me, and I guess, so I'm told anyway, that I just laid there and let him do it. That's when they decided that even though I wasn't 'out of it,' then I must have been looking for, and wanting, what was starting to happen. Well, from what they told me later, it went from just touching me to asking me if he could pull my warm-ups off. They told me I said, "Yeah", but I'm still not sure if I did or not! Seriously guys, I was there on that floor for about three or four hours and did not remember any of it, except for that real short time when I know somebody was feeling my ass. They said Mikey asked if he could take my warm-ups off, and I told him, "Sure". They said I even kind of helped him by raising up off of the floor some, so he could pull 'em off! Well, once the warm-ups were off, then I'm sure everything else came off too. I think I originally had on a pair of white briefs. Never saw them again! Those guys finally had me naked. They told me that whatever they did to me, I was all for it! They told me later, once we could calmly talk about what had happened, that all of them played with my dick, and for almost the entire time that I was laying there naked! I said I kept telling 'em to do it! They said they even asked me if they could measure it, and I told them, 'Yeah, do it!' Anyway, so they say! Seriously, some of those guys did convince me later that they truly thought I was totally with it. They told me that if at anytime they had thought I did not know what was going on, they would never have participated!"

"Participated? How did they participate? What did they do?" Jim anxiously asked as he continued to rub Jason's leg and slide his hand up and under his bag!

"Well from what I was told, they pretty well played with me, all parts of me! They told me I kept wanting it, and I was going for whatever they wanted. From what I was told later, I got my first blow job and my first ass fucking, and I still don't remember either one of them! They told me that four guys all fucked me, and one of those guys had never fucked a guy's ass before, but once everybody else was going for it, he decided to do it too. They said they even had a contest to see who could take most of my cock! I deep throated some guys that night, and don't remember any of it! And they told me I kept acting like this was stuff I did all the time!"

"My God man, what in the hell happened then? I mean you said earlier you woke up during your first time! What'd you mean by that?"

"Jack was on my butt, well really — he was up in my butt, a big man, a real big man, and Steve had sat down in front of my face, bare-assed as all outdoors, I might add, and he asked me if I wanted to suck his dick! They all said that I actually reached up for it and stuck it in my mouth! They swear, all of them do, that I was as much into getting stuff done to me, as they were instigating it! Well — it was while I was getting fucked in the ass by Jack, and I had Steve's dick stuck down my throat, that I actually came to, and realized what in the hell was happening! Steve's got a long dick, and I think what happened was that I started to gag on it, and that woke me up! I was not happy! I was pissed and mad as hell! I admit, I was still pretty well drunk, and if I had not been, I'm not sure just what in the hell I would have done. I was weak, and not walking or standing up too well. After a lot of talking, by all of the guys, they finally got me to understand they all thought I was wanting it! They actually were all convinced that during that whole time, I was all OK. I might have acted OK, but I was pretty well out of it! But then, that made me and the others start questioning just why in the hell was I so agreeable, if I was naturally, so all against it! That really made me wonder about me! And I thought, wait here a minute! I had Steve's dick down my throat, and if I hadn't agreed to do that, how in the hell could he have gotten it in so fucking far? I realized that when I came to, nobody was force holding me to do anything! I wasn't fighting to get Jack out of my ass nor was I fighting to get Steve out of my mouth!"

"Oh shit man, I can't believe this!" Bob stated. "Jason, obviously you found out sometime, that gay sex was OK! When did you decide that?"

"That night! Yeah, that night! Really guys, with all the talking that was going on in that room about what had happened, I started wondering if maybe I was, unconsciously, wanting it. Someone suggested that maybe, since I was there with other guys that, obviously, did not see a problem with gay sex, that maybe I should see if I liked it when I knew what I was doing.

After a little while of talking and trying to figure some shit out, I finally agreed to let some of them start touching me, just to see how I reacted. A couple of them came over to where I was sitting, and started touching my chest and finally letting their fingers rub up against my tits. I still didn't have any pants on, nor did anybody else, and everybody in the room saw my dick jerk when they first touched my tit! That encouraged all of them. I don't know if I was encouraged or not, but at least I was starting to know that I was not repulsed by having some other guy touch me. Finally, especially after watching my dick jerk some, I finally ended up with all of the guys touching me someplace on my body! One was on one tit, another on the other tit, one touching my dick, another touching my bag, shit man — there wasn't anyplace they weren't touching! I started accepting what was really happening, and finally asked one of the guys if he was one of the guys that sucked on my dick earlier and he said yeah, he was. I asked him to do it again! I was gay! When his mouth hit that dick, I knew I was gay! Or well — maybe Bi! But when he went down on that dick, I knew then that whatever happened earlier that night, was, internally within me, OK! I got so fucking rock hard when he went down on it, they told me it got bigger and stiffer than when they were playing with it before. There was a whole new celebration that night and it had nothing to do with my promotion! On my first night of knowing I was gay, or at least liked gay stuff, I found out all at once just which guys on the force were playing with guys! They added a new one that night! Me! Been doing it ever since!"

"Oh shit man, what in the world happened then. How did that night end? Everything end OK? I mean, I guess you weren't mad were you?" Bob asked seriously.

"Oh hey everything ended OK. Course it wasn't till about mid morning that things finally got ended. Thank goodness most of us had told our wives we were gonna be drinking so we were gonna stay at Joey's house for the night and not drive. We figured, all we needed was to have a whole bunch of State Troupers picked up for drunken driving! So anyway, being gone that long wasn't a problem. And, I've got to admit, it wasn't until that night that I actually found out that some of the women I knew, were not really wives, just girl friends that acted the wifey roll, when their gay cop friend needed a woman beside him! So anyway, after everything got all straighten out, and I found out about the real me, and the other guys finally got to see me, not only naked but with a major hard-on too, all of them wanted to try it on for size. First night knowing, and I was fucking four state cops! Oh that Jack guy, what a fuck! God was he good! He took it better than any of the rest! Fucked him probably five or six more times before I had to move! Damn his ass is good! I'd like to do that one again sometime!"

"Well Jason, what's your married life like now? Everything OK at home?" Jim asked with some very serious concern.

"Yeah, it's OK! Marge and I, Marge is my wife, we still do it once in awhile, but not nearly as often as I get it from guys! I kinda think she has some suspect that I do the sex thing outside of the house, someplace, but I don't know if she thinks it's with guys or not! I just don't make an issue about it. I just keep myself all primp and proper, so the guys will go for it, and the more the merrier! And I am really looking forward to adding both of you hot guys to my list of most desirables! Both of you guys play good! From what I've seen today, neither one of you guys are wimps! You both take it and give it rough, and that is what I like! And I'll be serious man, if I'm gonna fuck some guy's ass, he better be able to take it pretty rough, cause even if I go real easy, it can still feel pretty rough going up in there! My dick takes some room just getting up in there before much real fucking is going on! Now men — I need my ass fucked! I really do! Seriously men, way too many guys only want me for my dick, either to suck on it or take it up in their little shit chute, and I don't hardly ever get it in the ass. Guys, please, can I count on you guys to use my ass as well as my dick? Cole does pretty good, but his ass is always so fucking hungry, I just have to feed it. I figure, hey, he's letting me use his place for action, then I need to take care of him! But, man o'live, please — one of you guys, or both of you guys, please fuck me!"

"You sure don't have to beg me, man!" Bob strongly stated.

"Well, you sure can count on me going up in there too! Jason, you've got yourself two new puppies that are gonna love the hell out of you! I've heard of guys double fucking some guy, somehow or another, —maybe Bob and I can figure out how to do that, if you want!"

"Oh my God, yes! Oh shit man — hell yes! Yeah, I can show you guys how to do that! Wow, I really have hit the ole jackpot today! Guys, really, really, the idea of both of you guys up in my ass at once, oh shit man — I want that!"

Chapter Seven: Bite it Man, Bite it!

Returning back to the living room "play area", Bob suggested, "Hey Jason, I know damn well that Jim wants that pole of yours up in his ass again, so why don't we get started with you slamming his ass, and I'll poke you some. How's that sound guys?"

"Hey man, that sounds great to me!" Jason replied. "Yeah, let's do that. Jim, lay down there, and let me at it again. Seriously man, I really do think you're gonna like it better this time than when you just slammed down on it so fast before."

Jason grabbed some grease and greased his pole up, and smiled down at Jim, as Jim twisted his head back to watch Jason get his enormous rod good and greasy — and good and hard!

"Yeah, ready man? This time it's gonna be so much better than before. I want to go up in you just as far as I can, but this time, without your cute little white ass hurting any!'

Jim laid his head down and waited for the entry. He felt Jason's massive body lay down on top of him, and he felt the tip of Jason's rod touch right at his back door.

"Oh yeah man, oh yeah!" Jim exclaimed as he knew he was just about ready to get all of Jason's meat up inside of himself, and this time on a very caring and loving basis. "Yeah man, come on, fuck me, fuck me!"

Jason slowly started the entry by reaching up and massaging Jim's butt cheeks slightly, poking his fingers into Jim's little tight hole, and pulling the edges of it slightly open, so that it was real ready for the "real thing'.

"Oh man, poke me man, poke me! Jason, go in me. Fuck me! Fuck me please!"

"OK, OK! If that's what you want, I'll do it, if that's what you want! You really want me to just go in right away? You sure? That what you want?"

"Yeah man, yeah! Jason I need to feel you up in there! God, I need your dick man, I need it! Please just let me have it man, let me have it!"

Jason only said two words, "Hang tight!"

Immediately Jason let Jim have all of it! He had been told to slam his ass, and he checked to make sure Jim knew what he was saying, and he decided he did. He had asked for it that way, more than once. Jason went in! All the way! He slammed down into Jim's ass just about as fast as when Jim impaled himself on it earlier!

"Oh yes man, oh yes! Yeah, yeah — I love it man — I love it!" Jim yelled as he flipped his head back and forth in reaction to having his body suddenly filled with an enormous stick of thick, stiff, meat!

"You OK man, you OK?" Jason asked as he laid there with his "all" firmly planted up inside of Jim's torso.

"Oh yes, oh yes!" Jim quickly answered. "I'm more that OK! Jason, I love feeling that dick up in me! My God, my ass feels so good! This feels great! Oh I love feeling it up in me like that!"

Then attempting to turn his head far enough to talk to Bob, Jim asked, "Hey man, you fucking our buddy yet? He wants your dick in him, fuck him!"

Jason too looked around toward Bob and said, "Yeah man, yeah! He's right! I want your dick! Fuck me! I need it! I need to be fucked, and fucked good!"

As Jason was starting his actions on Jim's ass, as it had been begged for, Bob moved over on top of Jason's ass and placed his face right at the separation of the two magnificent, mahogany, muscular, ass mounds. Reaching up with both hands, he slid each hand up into the crevice that was so beautifully displayed right in front of his face. Slowly he let each hand slide up the entire length of Jason's ass crack and he slightly pulled each side open, ever so slightly, so that he could force his face down into the tight enclosure. His face cheeks and Jason's ass cheeks, were firmly planted, skin to skin!

"Oh wow! Wow!" Jason responded. "Oh man, that is great! Yeah man, I like that! Yeah, yeah, lick my ass, lick me!"

Jim, laying face down under both of the others asked, "Hey man, what's he doing? What's going on?"

"Oh man, he's got his face up in my ass! He's licking and biting my ass! Oh man, that feels so good! Oh Bob, I haven't had anybody's face in my ass like that in months! Yeah man, push your face in there man, yeah push it in!"

Bob continued to position himself so that he was definitely in a maximum position for grabbing both of Jason's butt muscles and pulling them in separate directions, so that he could manage to force his face as deep into Jason's ass crevice, just as far as possible!

As Bob managed to intrude closer and closer to Jason's asshole, Jason was pumping Jim's ass and consequently his ass was now moving up and down, as Bob was attempting to find the rose bud that he was now so determined to taste.

"Oh my God man, he's eating my ass man, he's eating my ass! Oh fuck man, you doing OK? You OK?"

Not realizing just which man Jason was addressing his question to, Jim responded, "Yeah man, yeah! Keep it up, keep it up, it feels good! Push deep real deep! Make me know I've got all of your dick!"

And at the same time, Bob pulled back just far enough to answer, "Oh yeah man, yeah, I'm doing fine. This is hot! Jim, his ass is hot shit man, hot shit! I never thought I'd ever have my face pushed up in some guy's back behind, but man o'live, this is fucking great! Oh, the feeling of his butt cheeks pushing back on my face is so fucking hot — damn this is good!"

Immediately Bob resumed his position of ass licking, kissing and sucking. He managed to get into a motion with Jason so that each time Jason raised up to slightly pull out of Jim's ass some, he managed to stick with Jason's ass, and as Jason slammed back into Jim's butt hole, Bob managed to slide with along with the motion and not loose touch of Jason's ass muscles, nor his position of aiming for Jason's sweet cherry.

Suddenly Jason stopped moving and thrust his ass up into the air and presented it fully and openly to Bob, and Jason said, "Hey Jim, I gotta stop here for a minute. I've gotta give your buddy, my ass to eat! He's tonguing my ass and I gotta let him do that for a minute, it feels so damn fucking good! He's got his face right in my ass! Yeah, eat me man! Eat me!"

Calmly laying there and enjoying the great feeling of having Jason's big dick up in his ass, he turned toward Bob's direction as fully as he could and asked, "Hey buddy, what you doing back there? You eating that bunch of strong black muscle ass out? You tonguing it? Eat it man, eat it!"

Bob pulled his face out just far enough to let his buddy, Jim, know just how great this new experience was. "Oh man, oh man! I have never stuck my face up in some guy's ass before, but man o'live, Jim, this sure ain't gonna be the last time. This is great! Oh man, just feeling his butt muscles pushing up against my face is so hot! Man I love this! This gives me a raging hard-on just pushing my face up in there! There's no way anybody could have convinced me earlier that I'd be licking and eating the asshole of some guy, but man, what an experience! And a state trouper no less! Oh hell man, I can't believe this man, I can't! Shit man, every time I see one of you guys out there on the highway with your tight fitting uniform pants on, grabbing your ass and grabbing your crotch, I'll probably just cum in my shorts, remembering this! God, I can't believe I've got my face up in a trouper's ass crack! And what a fucking ass crack! Hey Jason, buddy, am I doing this right? Can you feel my face up in there? This OK, man?"

"Oh shit hell yes man, it's OK!" Jason emphatically replied. "Bob my ass feels great! Eat me man, eat me! Get your teeth right up there right at my little hole and bite it man, bite it! Leave some bite marks on my ass. My wife ain't gonna see them up in there — give me some bite marks! Let me feel your teeth on my hole! Do me man, do me! I never get this — oh God, oh shit this is great! —Bite it man — bite it!"

Along with biting them and trying to give him some bite marks to take home with him, Bob immediately went back to eating and licking Jason's strong firm ass muscles and attempted to stick his tongue out far enough to slide it up, and into Jason's asshole, just even a little bit.

Jason kept giving Bob his ass, and did reach around and attempted to pull his butt cheeks open even farther, so that Bob could get his face up in there just as far as possible. Feeling Bob's face stuck up in his ass crack, and enjoying it to the fullest, he also started back in on Jim's hole! His body actions of slamming in and out of Jim, also forced his ass to slam back and forth onto, and off of, Bob's face.

"Jason, I gotta fuck you, I've gotta fuck you man!" Bob explained as he pulled his face out of Jason's butt and moved to get into position so that he could new use his dick in Jason's ass.

He quickly smeared some grease on his dick and without saying anything else, he pointed it at Jason's rose bud hole and went in! He was excited and anxious, and he did not waste any time going in!

"Oh God! Oh man!" Jason let out with a slight squeal. "Oh God man, how big is that little white pecker of yours? Damn man, that fucker sure as hell feels a whole lot bigger than it looks! Oh man, that kind of shocked me! Keep it up man, keep it up, I've got you in me now! It's OK now! Fuck me, fuck the officer! Oh shit Jim — when he fucks you, does he fill you up that much too?"

Not allowing Jim to answer, Bob jumped in, "Hey man — when I first fucked him, I don't even think he could feel it. I told him it was all the way up in him and he thought I was joking! I had to slam his ass to get him to know it was up in there."

"No man, I knew it was up in there, but you gotta remember I begged and begged for you to go up in me real slow and easy since I'd never had anything put up in there before."

"Well Jimmy little guy," Jason stated, "If you couldn't tell that dick of his was up in your ass, then you have got one hell of a hungry and open asshole back there. No wonder you slammed your ass down on my dick the way you did a little bit ago! Shit man, get a fucking 18 wheeler in here! Your ass can take just about anything that comes around, can't it?"

"No, I don't think so! Really, just having your big dick up in me is making me feel like my ass is all ripped up and ripped open. Really Jason, taking your dick is just about all I think I could take up in there. Yeah, I know when I jumped down on your dick earlier was pretty stupid, but man, I had dreamed of doing that, to that Al guy, for so many years, when I got the chance with you, I just had to do it! Now I know and realize I could have really done some shit to myself by doing that, and thank goodness I didn't, but I'm glad I did it! I needed to do it, and thank goodness I got to do it without tearing myself all up! I'll admit, I'll never do that again. Well, anyway, not on your fucking big dick, anyway!"

"Well! I'll tell both of you guys, my ass is feeling damn good now with Bob and his rod slammed up in there — but with me just knowing what it felt like when Bob slammed into me, I've still gotta wonder just how in the hell you managed to slam your ass down on my dick so fucking fast earlier. My ass feels good now, but for a minute, if felt like a bomb had gone off in there. But don't stop Bob! I like what's going on now, and it's feeling good! It's been way to long since I had some guy up in there, and I'm enjoying this, and it's feeling good! But Jim boy, how in the hell did you manage to take all of my dick without going crazy after you slammed it up in you? God man, your ass has gotta be one fucking tough ass!"

For at least the next 15 or 20 minutes, Jim continued to lay there on the floor with Jason on top of him, and into him about ten inches or so, and Jason continued to be the middle man, poking and fucking Jim's ass as he, himself, got it in the rear from Bob! All three men were living the life of luxury and total enjoyment!

"Jimmy, Jimmy, Jimmy" Jason suddenly exploded with, "Get ready man, get ready! I'm gonna cum, man I'm just about ready to let it fly, get ready, oh man — oh Jim! Oh shit man — I'm cumin in your little white asshole man — I'm cummmin!"

"Oh shit man, me too!" Bob then suddenly let out with excitement! "Oh shit man! Oh Jason! I'm about ready to feed your ass! I'm gonna feed your ass man, I'm about ready to cum! Jason, I'm gonna knock you up man, I'm gonna give you a kid! Oh man — here it comes — it's coming — it's commming! Oh shit man — I'm wiped out! Damn man, you have got one fucking hot ass! Let me tell you something! You sure aren't gonna have to worry about that asshole going empty very often. Jason, anytime you need it, or you want it, all you gotta do is let me know! Wow! Oh shit! Damn, that was good!"

As Bob got done telling Jason about how hot his ass was and how he was ready to fuck it any time Jason needed it, or wanted it, he realized that both Jim and Jason were laughing.

"Hey what in the hell you two laughing at? What's funny?" Bob asked, looking down at the two men underneath of himself.

"That you are gonna knock-up Jason! Bob, buddy, you are not fucking some gal! That's a man's ass you were unloading in, not some gal! I know you probably didn't realize just what you were yelling when you said that, but just picture yourself! You're on top of one hot looking muscular black state troupers, big man, big man — one that could pound the hell out of us both with one full swing, and as you're unloading in his ass, you're telling him, you're gonna knock him up!? You're gonna give him a kid! Don't think so, man — I really don't think so! You know what! Now that I think about what just happened and what you just said, I kinda think that if gay sex was a lot more accepted, there'd be less kids running around. Just think about it. A guy gets horny. He goes out and finds himself some other guy, fucks the hell out of him, dumps his load up in his ass, but no kid! I think there needs to be a law that guys can only fuck a woman when they are sure they want another kid! What you guys think?"

"Hey man!" Bob replied. "What I think right now is, that you are now, just wanting to find reasons to fuck guys, just as often as you can! Or maybe, knowing what kind of a smile you've had on that face of yours, the whole time you've had Jason's big rod up in you, maybe you wanna be the one to get fucked! Right?"

"Hey man, don't matter if I'm fucking or getting fucked, I'm into this shit man, I'm into it! Little did I know when I moved in across the street from Bob — how in the hell he was gonna change my life, but man — I'm really a different guy now than I was yesterday! Now my only question is — when are we gonna do this all over again? I gotta get home before Suzzie figures out something is going on, but I gotta know just when we can do you again? Seriously men, I'm gonna need this again real soon. I thought I went through a lot of changes yesterday, but today, playing with you today Jason, that is one hell of a lot more than I'm sure almost all gay guys can say they've ever done! How in the hell can I ever keep from telling everybody that I know, that Bob and I have got one of the hottest, best built, biggest muscular, hung like a horse, State Troupers, that we can come over and either fuck, or get fucked by, whenever we want? Muscles, muscles, and muscles, and one dick that could dam up the Mississippi, if it got in the way! Can't ask for anything better than that!"

On the Web!

"Hey guy — you ever just kinda cruise stuff on the web?" Jake asked his co-worker, and his buddy Ken, as they were sitting in Eddie's Northside Bar and Grill, having a couple, after work, brews before heading home for the night. Jake had suggested the idea of a couple of beers this night — if Ken had the time. Ken said yes, he did have the time, and they were now into their second beer each.

"Well yeah — I guess I do — sometimes. Not much, but yeah I have before. Why?"

Turning more directly toward Ken and leaning over toward him some, Jake answered. "I found some really weird stuff last night when I was just goofing around. Some stuff I've never seen before, but sure kinda woke me up some."

Looking very puzzled, Ken looked very seriously at Jake and asked, "What you talking about buddy? What'd you find?"

"Hey, tell you what! Let's finish these beers and get outta here. I think I brought up something I'm not too comfortable talking about in here. I'm afraid somebody'll hear me, OK?"

Now really looking very confused, Ken looked at Jake and just said, "Oh, well — OK!"

Ken and Jake were co-workers in a furniture warehouse. Jake was the original of the two employees at the warehouse, and Ken had joined the company about a year and a half before this conversation happened at Eddie's Northside Bar and Grill.

Although Jake was not the official company supervisor for Ken, he being a little older than Ken — he being 38, and Ken only being 25, but yet, one hell of a big six foot four, 234 pound, muscle bound, black man, the age difference had made Jake rather become an informal supervisor and advisor for Ken. He had rather taken over the roll as the "informal leader," of their work team.

With Ken now being very confused as to just what Jake was talking about, and Jake, in turn, now wondering if maybe he had bought up a subject that maybe he shouldn't have gotten into, they each finished their respective beers, sat the bottles down on the counter and after looking at each other with a rather, "You ready to go?" look, they each got up and headed for the door.

After getting outside and walking toward the parking lot, Ken finally looked over toward his work buddy Jake and asked, "So tell me guy, what in the hell were you talking about in there? What were you saying?"

"Hey guy, I don't know. I mean — I guess maybe now that I've started it, maybe it's something that I shouldn't have even brought up! Let's just forget about it! OK? OK?"

"No! Hell no!" Ken rather firmly, but yet laughingly, came back with. "No guy! You started something, now tell me what in the hell you were talking about! What'd you find on the web? What'd you see?"

After walking rather slowly toward his car, and now finally reaching it as Ken continued to press for an answer, Jake turned, leaned back and leaned on the trunk of his Chevy Malibu. Looking up toward Ken, since Ken was about three inches taller than himself, and he was now also leaning back onto the truck of his car, Jake finally took a deep breath and said, "I was just goofing around some on the computer, and I typed in something like, 'black men'. A whole bunch of stuff came up, and I just started opening some stuff I've never looked at before and I gotta be honest, I really didn't know that kinda stuff was that easy to find on the web. Stuff I never thought I'd see on some computer."

"You typed in something like — 'black men'? Is that what you just said?" As Ken turned, and he too leaned back onto the trunk of the car, he stood beside Jake and softly asked, "Jake, why in the world would you type in, 'black men,' on the search engine? Explain that one to me please!"

Ken's interest of just why Jake would use the words, 'black men', in his search, was very, very, certainly a strong point of interest —since, he, himself, was a black man, and Jake, his work buddy, the one that he just now found out had used the words, 'black men', in the search, was a white man!

"I don't know man, I don't know! I was just goofing around on the computer since I was home all alone and nothing else to do, and I just put in those words and stuff came up. A whole list of stuff came up and I started just opening up stuff, and the more I opened, the more shocked, but the more fascinated, I got. I've just never done that kind of stuff on the computer. I really didn't know that stuff was on there and was so fucking easy to find."

Asking rather emphatically, Ken asked, "Ken, what stuff? What'd you find? What'd you find — that you never thought you'd be finding?"

Kinda looking over toward Ken, but not directly into his face, Jake softly said, "Guys playing with each other! Guys having sex together! That stuff."

Looking toward Jake, even though Jake was rather looking down, Ken stated, "Uh — wait a minute here guy! You found some gay sites? You found some gay sex on line?"

"Yeah, yes I did! Ken, I had no idea that stuff was on line! I didn't!"

"Wait, wait, wait! Let me ask this again! Why did you use the words 'black men'? Jake, I'm finding this rather curious! You use 'black men' as your search words, then end up finding and watching, gay sites!? Were there black men in those gay sites?"

"Yeah, yeah — some of 'em were. Yeah."

All of a sudden, a lot of things were now going through Ken's head. 'Why, just why in the world would Jake have gotten on the internet and used the words, 'black men,' and then ended up looking at gay sites? He knows I'm single, he knows I'm black — was it me he was kinda thinking about when he chose those two words? What was he really wanting to find on there? Why was he maybe thinking about me when he did that?'

"Hey Jake! When you sat down at that computer, what was on your mind man, what were you thinking about?"

"Nothing, I don't think man, nothing! I was just trying to pass some time, and I just typed in 'black men' and then all these web sites came up, and I of course started clicking on some of 'em."

"And you ended up finding some gay sites — right?"

"Yeah, yeah I did. I didn't know that's what they were until I opened a couple of 'em and then I realized what they were."

"Uh- so what'd you do then?"

"Ken, I was shocked, and yeah, I looked at some of 'em. Maryanne and the kids weren't home, they're at Grandma's this week, and since there wasn't anybody there, I went ahead and looked at some of 'em."

"So, what'd you think? What happened?"

"I don't know, I don't know!"

"Jake, what do you mean, you don't know? What'd you think, what'd you do?"

"Ken, I guess I musta been kinda fascinated. I didn't stop. I looked at some of 'em."

"So, what'd you look at?"

"Well, some of 'em were just some guys, guys together, but not doing nothing, really. Well touching each other, but that's all."

"So just some still shots?"

"Well yeah. But then I clicked on some ad thing, and then a video came up and actually showed guys sucking on each other and on one, a guy was getting fucked in the butt. Ken, I didn't know that stuff was that easy to get to, I didn't!"

"So, like how long did you look at it? How long were you on there?"

"Ken, I ended up watching a lot of it. I didn't go to bed till after midnight. I just kept having more and more sites keep coming up, and yeah, I looked at 'em."

"So tell me! You typed in 'black men', right?"

"Yeah I did! That's what started this whole thing."

"So Jake, let me ask you again. When the words 'black men' came to your mind, were you thinking about me? You had to have some reason to use those two words, and I just can't help but think that since you were home all alone, you were thinking about me, or somebody like me, and you decided to see what you could find on the internet since you were home all alone, right?"

Rather embarrassed, Jake slightly looked up toward Ken and admitted, "Yeah Ken, yeah I will admit it, I was. I've kinda wanted to see if I could see some black guys on the web to see if what everybody says about you guys, is right or not."

"'What, everybody says about us guys', right? You mean, like everybody says we've got big long 'slongers', right? That what you're saying?"

"Yeah, yeah that's right."

"And so—, what'd you find out?"

"Ken, I don't know, I don't know."

"Why? Didn't you see any of the black guys hanging out? Letting their stuff show? Gay sites — you had ta" have seen some black dick, didn't yea?"

"Hey, yeah, I did, but Ken — they're only gonna show the really big guys on something like that aren't they? Yeah, those guys were all hanging big stuff, but Ken, really — those porno sites are gonna just show the big stuff, aren't they?"

"So I think I'm finally getting my answer to my question about if you were maybe thinking about me when you typed in 'black men'. Right? Right?"

"Yeah, yeah — yeah Ken I was. Ever since you came to work with me, I've always wondered about it, and I've always wondered if what they say, is true or not. Yeah, yeah Ken, I was thinking about you when I did that search. I was just wondering if I could finally get my big question answered by looking at some other guys, but I sure didn't expect to find the stuff I did! Yeah, I saw some dicks, but I gotta be honest, I really doubt those are the average guys. I'm just sure all those guys are on there cause they do have big dicks!"

"So did you like looking at the dicks that you did see? What'd you think about them?"

"Hey Ken, maybe we'd better just kinda drop this conversation. I might'a brought up something that I should've never mentioned. OK?"

"Looking over toward his buddy, his co-worker, and after this conversation, probably his now much closer friend than they had been only a few minutes ago, Ken firmly stated, "No! No, we're not dropping this conversation! Maybe I think we're finally into a conversation that I've been wanting and praying for, for the last year or so."

"What!? What'd you mean by that? What'd that mean, Ken?"

"Jake, you had guts to tell me what you saw on the internet last night, and probably early this morning before you headed out for work too, and now I'm gonna be real gutsy and tell you — that Jane I used to date was really John, and that Rachel was really Richard. Jake — I don't date girls, I date guys! I've wanted you and me to have this kind of a talk ever since I met you and saw you in those tight uniform pants you wear. Don't let anybody see you, but try and look down and look at the rod you're showing right now! Jake, for a more than a year now, I've kept my mouth shut and never said anything, but I've wanted to see what in the hell you've got packed in there, ever since the very first time I saw it! Every time I see you coming toward me, I check that crotch out and I swear man, it's getting bigger and bigger the longer I know you. There — now just who in the hell is wondering about who? You been wondering about us black brothers, and I've been wondering about you, just as much! Man, I wish I'd been there last night while you were looking at those web sites! Shit I wish I'd been there! Maybe I'd finally been able to see just what you been packing in there in front of me all the time!"

"Ken — you are gay, right? You are gay?"

"Yeah man, yeah! I told you, I've been lying about who I'm dating. Yeah man, I am. Finally, it's out! I've wanted you to know it ever since I started working with you, but I was afraid you wouldn't like me or work with me if I told you. Is it OK with you? Please tell me it's OK?"

"Looking over at Ken, Jake answered. "Hell yeah man, hell yeah it's OK!" Then, while rather shaking his head some, Jake continued, "You know man, I've wondered about you since day one, and I guess wondering about you last night just was what made me see what I could find on the internet. Suppose I was really hoping I'd end up finding a picture of you on there? I know that's impossible, but right now, I'm really wondering if I really was praying that I'd find some picture of you on there."

"Hey Jake, if you knew the right place, and you were a member of that site, yeah, you could've found me and my dick! Let's face it man, all of us horny guys are showing our stuff on the internet just hoping to make some connection with some hot guy, but — you gotta know the where and the how to find it. You've got a wife and kids at your house, I'm not so sure you need to be putting stuff like that up on your computer. Right?"

"Uh yeah, yeah I agree — but Ken, how can I see yours sometime? I mean, hey — if you're gonna put it on the internet for others, from all over, to see it, can I see it sometime? Can you show me what you've got on the web?"

"Hey man, let me figure you out here a little! You maybe a little more interested in stuff more, than just finding out if what you're told is true or not? Was that maybe just an excuse to tell me you've been seeing and watching some sites of guys doing it with each other?"

"Ken, I guess, yeah—yeah you're right! I've wanted to see you all stripped down ever since very shortly after we met. Ken, I've never wondered about some guy before, but I gotta admit, with you — I watched you bend over and pick up stuff, and I've watched you reach your hands up over your head and reach for stuff, and Ken — yeah, I gotta be honest with you since you've finally told me you're a gay guy, I'd love to see you — naked I guess! Yeah, I've finally told you, I wanna see what you look like with nothing on — well maybe just some briefs."

"Well — just maybe some briefs on!? Come on man, you gotta be kidding! You don't want me having no briefs on if I get that close! 'Sides, man, I don't ever wear briefs! They hold stuff up too tight! I gotta let mine kinda hang loose! You wanna see it? You wanna see my slonger, right? You wanna see it?"

"Uhhhh, yeah, yeah I do! Oh gawd Ken, I can not believe I'm telling you this! This don't make me sick or weird if I admit it does it? Is it OK that I'm telling you this?"

Leaning over slightly toward Jake, Ken states, "Jake my man! Jake I'm a gay guy! You wanna see my slonger, and I've been wanting to see yours for a long time! You think I'm gonna call you a sickie if you admit you wanna see what I'm hanging? Hell no! I wanna see what you're hanging too! Hey, you said your wife and the kids are out of town this week, right?"

Looking directly at Ken with a smile on his face, Jake replied, "Yeah — yeah they are. Does this maybe mean what I'm hoping it means? This mean maybe you're thinking we can get together so I can see your dick and see how big it is?"

"Hey man, sure works for me, I wanna do it too. Got time tonight to come over ta my place for a little while before you go home?"

"Yeah Ken, yeah I do, but hey — how about if we go to my place, just in case Maryanne and the kids calls. I'll be there to answer the phone. Can we do that? I'd feel better being at my place. OK?"

"Hey works for me! This is gonna let me find out once and for all if everything that I think might be in there, really is. Should I follow you, or you wanting me to come over later tonight?"

Still leaning up against his car, and looking down toward Ken's crotch, Jake kinda, unconsciously, licked his lips ever so slightly, and then replied, "No, follow me. Ken, I'm afraid if I don't go through with this right now, I'm afraid I'll back out. I wanna see it, but man, I'm fucking nervous about doing this. I've never done anything like this before, seriously man, I never have. Come on, let's go before I change my mind and end up saying no."

Quietly and without further words, Ken and Jake got into their respective cars, and for the next ten minutes Ken followed Jake to his house. Even during the drive, Ken was excited and had to, more than once, reach down and readjust his enlarging rod, and move it into a much more comfortable space. Never had he ever imagined that Jake was maybe interested in just how well he was built nor how big he was hung. For more than a year now, the two had been working together, side by side. And even though he, Ken, had been checking out Jake's crotch and kinda imagining just what was tucked inside that was so nicely creating that larger than usual bulge in his basket, never had he entered the thought that maybe, just maybe, Jake was as interested, or even more interested, in just what he was packing. Now, he decided, he finally knew the real reason that Jake had asked if he'd like to stop on the way home from work and have a beer. The whole little situation, Jake's interest in Ken's dick, was obviously the reason that made Jake get on the internet and type in the two words, 'black men.'

As they drove slowly through a housing neighborhood, headed toward Jake's house, all of a sudden Ken did realize that earlier that day, Jake had made a rather weird comment about the baggy pants some of the younger guys were wearing lately, and how disgusting they looked. He had made a comment about how in the hell can anybody see just how they're built if they dress that way. Never before, had Jake ever made any comments even close to that! Ken, all of a sudden, realized that when Jake had made that comment, he had found it to be a very off base comment or observation for Jake. He did remember back that he, himself, Ken, had mentally thought, 'Well Jake my man! With what I think you must be hiding inside of those pants, thank goodness you don't wear anything that loose! I like looking at that bulge you're showing! Just keep yours kinda tight. Looks good man, looks good!' Never had he ever heard Jake make any type of a comment about anything even close to this comment — about not knowing how some guy was built.

As Jake parked his Chevy in the drive, Ken pulled in beside him, parked his car, and the two men went into the house through the side door. Once inside, Ken looked around slightly, and made a pleasant comment about how nice the house was. "Hey man, this is nice, really nice!"

"Thanks man, thanks!" Jake replied. Then added, "Ken — I'm really afraid I messed up here man. Driving over here I really got to thinking, I must be out of my mind telling you about me getting on the web last night. I don't know what in the hell I thought I was doing when I told you about it, but Ken, I must'a been out of my mind. I'm sorry you drove over here. Really man, I can't go through with this. The idea of me looking at your dick is just wrong, it's just really wrong!"

Now leaning back against the kitchen counter that Ken had been standing close to, he commented, "Hey man! I wouldn't say that! What's so wrong with looking at something that obviously you've had some interest in for some time. I think this whole thing is turning out pretty well for us. I gotta be real fucking honest that I'm glad that this whole thing came up! It finally gave me a good reason to finally quit lying and finally just tell you I'm a gay guy. Jake, I've wanted you to know that ever since we met, but I was afraid to tell you. Now it's out in the open, and I'm glad! I know, big muscled built guys like me just aren't supposed to be gay guys, but the truth is — yeah, —some of us are! Jake, now that you know the real me, now I can finally tell you I wanna see just what you've got in your pants. That bulge in there has had my interest since day one. Come on man, come here, let me see it, OK?"

Still acting very confused and quite nervous about the conversation that he had gotten started, Jake silently stood there with a rather concerned look on his face. Ken leaned forward from the counter, reached out toward Jake, unbuckled Jake's belt, unbuttoned the five buttons on his pants, pulled the waist band of the pants down slightly, slid his finger tips into the top elastic of Jake's briefs, and then pulled 'em down, ever so slightly.

Jake did not move! Ken moved very slowly and very deliberately so that he would not scare Jake into begging off from being — "de-pantsed".

As Ken made his moves very slowly, Jake managed to look down to see just what Ken was doing, and as he saw his own dick come popping out of his briefs and showing a very major hard on, he heard Ken gasp, "Oh my gawd man — shit man — that is nice man! That is fucking nice! Oh look man — uncut! Jake, you've got one hell of a hot dick man, one hell of a hot dick!"

Jake stood there in somewhat of a state of shock, now realizing that he had just let some other man — one hell of a hot looking, well muscled built younger man, take his dick out of his pants and that young man was now holding it, feeling it and rubbing his hard on. He could not only see, but he could also feel Ken moving his hand back and forth — back and forth, along the entire length of his now stiff shaft. Sliding the foreskin back and forth, back and forth! For a very slight second, he closed his eyes and imagined the many, many times that he had done that same thing to himself, building his body to an eventful and an exciting, cum filled, shooting climax! Never, never, in his entire life had he ever had this happen, with some other man's hand, doing the rubbing. All of a sudden, he realized that even when his doctor had touched his dick or his bag, never had his dick been standing straight out, all puffed up, stiff and hard like it was right then! As he thought about that, he felt even more blood rush into his dick and he felt it get even stiffer and stronger. Once again he heard Ken utter, "Oh my gawd man — shit man — that is nice man! That is fucking nice!"

Jake could feel the warmth of Ken's big strong hand, massaging back and forth on his cock! Back and forth, back and forth, and with each movement, his rod felt more and more of the strength and warmth that Ken was now passing on to him. He liked what he was feeling, and he realized that for some unknown reason he was licking his own lips as he watched Ken keep a very keen eye on his dick, the actions that he was giving it, and noticing how Ken was seeming to slip into some type of a mysterious stance, as he slowly but very firmly continued to rub his dick and squeeze it harder and harder with each movement. Jake admitted to himself that he was experiencing a totally new and great dynamic sexual feeling, that he had never, never, had before. Never had he ever thought about what it could feel like to have another man jerk himself off — that was — until the night before, when he found, rather by mistake, some very active and some very exciting, gay, web sites.

As Jake stood there, his arms hanging down to his sides, his face looking down, sternly watching Ken manhandle his cock, and now rather subconsciously pushing his mid section out toward Ken, as if to offer it for service, he suddenly realized how exciting those gay sites on the web actually had been. He actually realized that when he had typed in the words 'black men," he truly had to have been subconsciously thinking about Ken, and very subconsciously hoping that something like this could, some day, happen between 'em. Suddenly he had the realization that internally, he had been putting this all together, and in his active, conscious real life, he had managed to get it set up, even though he was still trying to say, 'No, I can't do this!'

Ken's kind of slow, careful movements were becoming almost too much for him to contain any longer. Suddenly he let loose of Jake's thick and stiff rod, let loose of the waist band that he had still been holding onto with his left hand, and suddenly he dropped down onto his knees, threw his hands onto the upper sides of Jake's legs, threw his mouth wide open, and immediately took the entire eight and a half inches of his work buddy's stiff cock down and into the depths of his throat! Jake lurched forward, pushing his body toward Ken and at the same time grabbed a hold of Ken's head with both hands. "Oh yes! Oh yes!! Oh yes!!!" The words suddenly came, almost yelling, out of Jake's mouth! Even as a surprise to himself! He did not expect to have this action feel so unbelievably good! So unbelievably great — so unbelievably exciting! Being sucked on like this was a completely new and great experience. Something he had never experienced before! He was experiencing an entire body sensation, throughout his entire body, that he had never before felt! He planted his feet squarely on the floor, he grabbed on tight to Ken's head, and he thrust his torso out as strongly as possible, offering his man stick to his sucker friend!

Having heard the glorious words of, "Oh yes! Oh yes!! Oh yes!!!" being expounded and emphasized from above his head, Ken knew that what he was now sucking on and swallowing as deeply as he could, was the right thing to do, even if Jake had tried to beg off earlier. He knew Jake had lost all control! He was over the edge, and was begging for more and more! He grabbed tighter onto the sides of Jake's legs and pulled him even tighter and stronger toward himself so that he could take every small, partial bit of Jake's delicious white meat! Pushing his face into Jake's mid section, and pulling Jake's dick into his mouth as completely as he could manage, Ken had to breath through his nose. His entire mouth and throat, deep into his throat, was fully filled with his work buddy's dick — the dick that, only moments ago, he had managed to see out in the open for the very first time. The same dick that he had wondered about for more than a year, wondering just how much dick there was stuck into those work pants that made 'em stick out so far in the front. For a year or more, Ken would look down at his own crotch, just wondering if he managed to show as much manhood, "down there," as his white buddy was showing — and, on purpose or not! Ken had been complemented many times, usually by other gay guys, about what a great basket he showed, and for this entire year plus, Ken did have some little, fragmented, concerns that just maybe, just maybe, his white, older buddy was really managing to hold and show a little more manhood, down in the crotch area, than he was himself.

As he continued to suck all of the juices out of it as he could manage, Ken had to admit to himself that with what he had stuck in his mouth right then, did deserve to show itself as much and as often as it could. He knew that when he slammed his mouth onto it, it must have measured at least a good thick eight and a half inches long, but being a man that has sucked and chewed on a number of fortunate nine, ten and even eleven inch cocks, he knew this rod had to have reached at least a nine or nine and a half inch length. The extra length that it had managed to reach out to, once it was being sucked on, was great, but Ken had to admit that with the width of it and its enormous girth, Jake was actually giving him one of the most complete mouthfuls of cock, that he had ever taken. 'Thank God I can breath outta my nose!' was Ken's major thought, as he realized, over and over, just how stuffed full his entire mouth and throat were with one hunk of meat, that he had never seen before, but had been working right beside for about a year and a half.

Ken's head was moving back and forth, on and off of Jake's rod at an almost lightening speed. Jake was doing everything he could to help, or at least in his spinning mind help, by continuing to grab Ken's head and fucking it as fast and as furiously as he could, by pushing and pulling it on and off of his steel rod of a dick! He was experiencing a tremendous feeling of sex like he had never felt — once he had shot his first shot of cum, the very first time he jacked off! He had remembered that little jack off session, out behind the family barn, many, many times, and had wished each and every time he either had a jerk off session, or even a straight guy intercourse session with either his wife or earlier with a girl friend, that he could feel the same excitement that he felt that very first time he let his seeds fly out, of what was to him at that time, was the stiffest and hardest dick that any man, or young boy, could possibly have. He remembered how, as that cum flew out of him the very first time, it felt like he had just had a dam break in a wild flowing river! His body was finally getting back, that same original unbelievable, sexual feeling!

As he stood there, fucking the hell out of Ken's mouth, he realized that yes, he was finally getting that same great feelings that he had that sunny August afternoon, out behind the barn. His body was giving him every possible bit of excitement that it could muster, and he knew that in only a moment or two, he was going to be feeding Ken, his hot looking, muscled, handsome, tall, shaved head black stud of a work buddy, a mouth full that was gonna be one of his biggest loads of hot creamy cum that he had ever shot! His body was getting tight, it was getting rigid, and he was grabbing onto Ken's head like it would fall off if he let loose of it. He yelled, "Ken — Ken — Ken!!!!!" That was all he could manage to utter. He could not manage to put a sentence together, the simple yelling of Ken's name, was the optimum of what he could do! He knew that he has lost all self control of his entire being! Everything of him, and by him, was now completely rapped up in his dick and Ken's mouth!

With his mouth and his throat fully full, and being able to breath, only slightly, and just through his nose, Ken knew what that meant, and he managed to utter a, "Yeah, yeah," back to Jake. He jerked his head up and down as much as possible trying to tell Jake to, "Let it fly man — let it fly!!!" He knew — he could tell from the body movements of Jake's, and the way Jake's body had tightened up, as well as the way Jake had a hold of his head, and was fucking his mouth as fast and as feverishly as he was, he knew Jake was definitely very close to letting everything, and anything, that he had stored up inside of himself, and especially inside of his dick and his bag, to come flying out! And, Ken knew that he had better start swallowing the very second that he first felt some warm, hot, creamy, juices hit the back of his throat! Ken knew from the way Jake had been acting, for the last minute or two, that he was getting damn, damn, close to exploding, and when the first little bit of explosion hit, it was not gonna stop any time soon! He knew that Jake was in the middle of a body excitement that he had not had for years and years, and he knew that within just the few minutes that he had been sucking on Jake's stiff stick of meat, Jake had probably built up more cum and juices than he had totally, over the entire last month or so. He knew Jake was totally out of it! He knew he was giving his co-worker something more than words could tell. He felt Jake's sexual excitement just by having a hold of his body, and feeling how tense and tight it had gotten. He was glad he was the man, eating this dick, and he was glad he was the man that was going to be choking in a moment, on some cum that he knew was going to have to be some of the sweetest cum, he had had in his mouth in a long, long, time.

"Oh my gawd! Oh my gawd! Oh my gawd!" Was all that Jake could manage as he locked his body, his dick, and Ken's head together as he let it all fly! With every shot of explosion busting out of the end of his dick, Jake grabbed a hold of Ken's head that much tighter, and kept yelling, "Oh my gawd! Oh my gawd! Oh my gawd!" Each yell was louder and stronger! And with each yell and with each spurt of cum, he threw his body and his dick that much stronger at, and into Ken's mouth!

"Oh Ken! Oh Ken!" Jake calmly stated as he slightly let loose of Ken's head and slightly started to pull back on his body in an attempt to release his dick from the tight confines of, and the depths of, Ken's mouth! "Oh Ken, oh man! Oh shit man, what a fucking feeling! Oh man — oh man that was good! Oh Ken, I did not know getting it sucked on like that could feel that fucking good! Ken, Ken — you OK guy, you OK? Oh man, oh man! I've never blown a wad like that before! Ken, I've never had it explode out of me like that before! Oh my dick! Oh man, it feels so funny right now! Oh it feels like it just went through a tornado or something. Oh Ken it feels great! Oh Ken, it feels beat! Oh my dick, my dick — oh man it feels so fucking good right now, it feels so good!"

Taking a deep breath and licking some left over extra cum from the edges of his mouth, Ken pulled back some and licked the tip of Jake's dick and slid the tip of his tongue under Jakes' foreskin and licked it clean. Jake shivered and rather jerked at the warm sensitive feeling. Then, letting it slip out of his mouth completely, Ken looked up at Jake and said, "Oh shit man, wow! Damn man, you were sure as hell ready for that! Wow—you loaded my mouth and throat like it ain't been loaded in years! Jake, damn man — thank gawd you looked at some web sites last night! Damn man, what a dick! Shit man, how long's it been since you had a climax? Damn — you must have shot a full quart of juice into me man! Damn man, you really let it all fly! Man — what'd you do last night while you were looking at those pictures? You jerk on your dick and build up some extra cum? God man, your bag had to be full of cum, real full of cum! Man — what a mouthful you gave me!"

"Oh Ken — oh shit man — what can I say? Damn man, that felt so fucking good! Ken guy — that ain't gonna be the last time you ever do that to me, let me tell you that! Damn, you suck like a son of a bitch! Damn that felt good! Oh yeah man, Oh yeah! Here, suck on it some more for me, please!"

With Ken still on his knees on the floor in front of Jake, he heard the request, and he responded. He pointed Jake's still rock stiff cock directly at his mouth, and again completely swallowed it! Completely, fully and suddenly!

"Yeah man, yeah! Oh yeah Ken, oh yeah! Yeah man that feels good, that feels good! Suck me man, suck me!"

For the next ten minutes Ken continued to kneel there in place, and suck on Jake's dick. At the same time he was also reaching down, and even though he still had his own pants on, fully covering his own stick, he was rubbing his own hard-on. His own internal sexual excitement had definitely been highly aroused with the dramatic climax that he had just helped Jake explode with. He was getting very, very, close to wanting and needing the same thing to happen to him and to his dick!

Pulling off of Jake's rod, Ken looked up and asked, "Hey man. Can you do me? I mean, I gotta either get mine sucked on or I gotta at least jerk it off. I gotta cum, I gotta! You wanna suck on me, or should I jerk it off? I gotta pound it man, I gotta pound it!"

"Oh Ken, oh shit man! Oh man — I never thought about me sucking off some guy. Oh shit! Oh Ken, I gotta, I gotta. You did me, I gotta do you! I can't just let you do me and let me feel everything. I gotta do you! Oh man, I never thought about me putting my mouth on some guy's dick and having him fuck my face! But man, I gotta though, I gotta! I can't just have you doing me and me not trying to help you out too! You gotta help me though, you're gonna have to be patient with me, OK? Can you? Seriously man, I never thought about this before. Oh Ken — Ken, you think I can do it?"

"Hey buddy, it's up to you! It's up to you! If you would, I'd sure like it, but I'm not gonna force you into anything that you're not comfortable with. I will tell you one thing though, if you don't want to, that's OK but I've gotta jerk it off then! I gotta shoot man — I've gotta shoot!"

As Ken was telling Jake that he just had to shoot, he stood up, unbuckled his belt, unbuttoned his pants and after unfolding the waist band, started pulling 'em down. Jake stood there and with full, complete, attention he watched his buddy pull his pants down and let his big long black, uncut rod, come flying out!

"Oh my God man! Oh my God! Oh shit man, oh shit!" Jake exploded as he finally saw his co-workers rod come bouncing out! "Oh Ken, what a fucking dick! Ken, I've never seen a dick like that before! I've never seen a black man's dick before, and look how fucking big and stiff that thing is!

Yeah! Yeah Ken, I gotta admit that's the rod that made me get on the web last night and type in 'black men'! I was wondering what yours looked like and I looked at some on the web and wondered if any of them was like yours! Oh, you're is bigger, I swear it's bigger! Oh Ken, I gotta feel it, I gotta feel it, I gotta!"

After stepping out of his shoes and pulling his pants off, he moved over toward Jake and watched as Jake very nervously reached out, and slowly, placed his left hand on Ken's hot, stiff, pole.

"Oh Ken — Ken, this is so big! Ken, I can't get my hand wrapped around it! Oh Ken, this is unbelievable man! —This is fucking unbelievable! Oh Ken, this is like a big beer can man, it's like a big beer can! Oh I've never had a hold of another guy's cock before. Oh gawd man, this one is so fucking big! Oh Ken, you are hung like a fucking elephant man — a fucking elephant!"

As Jake grabbed onto Ken's stiff stick of meat, Ken placed his hand on top of Jake's hand, and started moving both of their hands back and forth! Jake watched what was happening, and then he looked directly into Ken's eyes. Eye to eye, the two men intently looked at each other. Ken sped up the motion that, now the two men, were enacting on his warm, stiff, dick. Both men, together, were jerking Ken off!

Continuing to first look directly at Ken, and then look down at Ken's dick and watch how he and Ken were stroking it back and forth and then looking up again at Ken's face, Jake said, "Ken, I gotta do this, I gotta do this! I gotta try to do this, I gotta try!"

After looking at Ken and telling him how he, "had to do this," Jake knelt down, leaned forward and put the tip of his tongue on the end of Ken's long black rod. He licked it softly back and forth, as he and Ken both continued their massaging of it as he then leaned forward farther and put his mouth on the head of the big thick dick, that he was so anxiously looking at and feeling. He slapped it back and forth about three times letting it hit him up beside his face. That made it get even bigger and harder! He took three big deep breaths! And then he took another three deep breaths through his nose. He plastered his gaze onto the big stiff black dick that he now had in his hand, and the same dick that earlier, he had thought, that he'd never even get a chance to see.

Ken quit stroking back and forth and then removed his hand so that Jake had complete control of his dick and what was happening to it! He was allowing Jake to manhandle it anyway he so desired! His work buddy was finally, finally, playing with his dick, and he liked it! He was excited that he and Jake were finally doing this! He had been wanting this to happen for a long time! He was excited that they were finally getting to know each other in this, one on one, fashion. A sexual way! And a hot sexual way! Ken was wanting to ram his rod down into the back of Jake's throat as far and as fast as he could! He was really wanting to just grab a hold of Jake's head, hold it firm and steady, and suddenly force all of his rod into that warm moist mouth, just as fast as he could! He wanted to, but he knew he had to let Jake take it at his own speed! He did not want to mess up the great activity and interchange that was now, finally, happening.

"Yeah man, yeah! Yeah I want you to do it Jake, I want you to do it! I've wanted you to do this ever since the first day we met! Jake, do it man, do it! Just take your time, but do it for me please! I wanna watch you suck on me man, I wanna watch! I wanna know you've sucked on me man, I wanna know you've done it! Everyday we go to work, I wanna know you've sucked on my dick! I wanna be able to just kinda close my eyes and see you sucking on my dick! I wanna work beside you knowing that you've chewed on my dick and that you've had my dick in your mouth! Do me man, please suck and chew on it! Take my dick!"

Slowly, and with more caution than Jake had ever experienced doing anything before, he opened his mouth as widely as he possibly could, and slowly took the head of Ken's massive big, black, stiff, rock hard dick into his mouth! Ken could feel Jake's tongue slide around the edge of it. "Oh yeah man, oh yeah! Oh Jake, that's good man, that's good! You OK? You doing OK? Oh yeah man! Oh yeah! Do it man, do it!"

Looking up toward Ken's face with only his eyes, keeping his face pointed directly forward, Jake tried to let his massive hunk of beef know that he was OK. Slowly he pushed forward, forcing ever so little more of Ken's big massive, stiff, hard rod into his mouth, and with his right hand, reach up and grab Ken's bag of big nuts and slightly pulled 'em down. Not really realizing just what he was doing, he was using Ken's bag of nuts as a handle to pull Ken toward himself, so that he could manage to take small bits of his dick farther into his mouth. It was definitely gagging him, he was choking, but he was determined to go down on it just as far as possible! He was suddenly realizing that he was now on his hands and knees, and he actually did have the tip of another man's dick in his mouth. Even the night before, while he was cruising the web, and watching other men suck on other guys, did he ever have the slightest imagination that within only one day, he would be doing the same thing. The mental image of him, kneeling down in front of Ken, grabbing on his legs, pulling him forward and trying to put as much of Ken's big black dick into his mouth was almost more than he could realize was really happening!

"Oh yeah, oh yeah!" Ken slightly uttered as he felt Jake's warm mouth cover over his ragging hard-on and at the same time feel his nuts being slightly pulled. "Oh yeah man, oh yeah! Yeah, squeeze my nuts man, squeeze my nuts! That feels so good! Oh man, yeah, do it, do it! Oh Jake you know what you're doing man, you know how to do it!"

"No I don't know, no I don't," was all Jake could think at that time. "There is no way in hell that I know what in the hell I am doing right now! I'm down in front of a man, he's got a fucking big boner sticking out at me, and I'm trying to put as much of it as I can, in my mouth! How in the hell did this happen? How in the hell did I start doing this? Oh shit man, oh shit! I'm sucking on some man's dick! I'm not supposed to be doing this! How in the hell did this all get started? Oh shit man, what in the hell am I doing?"

"Hey Jake, you OK man, you OK?" Ken asked as he smiled a big broad smile looking down at his co-worker, and his now much closer friend. "You doing OK? You like this?"

Jake attempted as much as possible to let Ken know he was "OK", but in his mind, he was still trying to sort out just what in the hell was happening here, and just what in the hell was he doing here! He knew he had wanted to see Ken's dick, see it — see how big it was — but he had never thought about maybe doing anything like putting his mouth on it! "Am I OK? He asked me if I'm OK! Shit man, am I OK? How in the hell am I supposed to know if I'm OK or not? Crap man, I'm not supposed to be OK doing this! Men ain't supposed to be doing this to each other! Shit man, why ain't I screaming that I am not OK? Why am I trying to make Ken think I'm OK if I'm not? What in the hell is going on here? If I'm not so OK, why in the hell am I trying to get more and more of his big black dick down in my throat? Why? Why is this kinda like OK with me if I'm not supposed to be doing it or liking it? I'm supposed to be real sick doing this, ain't I!? I should be screaming mad that he's making me do this to him. Wait— wait— he's not making me do it! He's not making me do it! He said if I can't do it, that's OK, he'd just beat it off! He's not making me do it — I'm doing it on my own. I agreed to do it! And I guess maybe I'm OK or anyway, kinda OK, or I wouldn't be doing it! Come on man — am I OK, or am I not? Decide, man, I gotta decide! I'm not getting sick doing it, and besides, I never thought some guy's dick could taste like this, nor feel this warm in my mouth! I'm not so repulsed doing this as I thought it would be if a guy did this to another guy! I thought this was supposed to be really repulsive! It's not! It's not at all! Oh man, oh shit, I'm starting to think maybe I like doing this, I think I am! He did me and I almost screamed in joy while he was doing me. I thought I was in heaven when I came! I sure as hell liked it when I was getting sucked on! I remember I said I had to do him, to pay him back! OK, so now I'm doing it! Yeah, I'm doing it, and face it idiot, I'm liking it — I'm fucking liking it man, I am! Yeah, I am! He tastes good and I guess I really do like the way he's up there, towering over me and feeding me his dick! I've got his dick in my mouth and I'm liking it! Oh shit man, I never thought I'd ever be telling myself anything like this! Yeah man, maybe I'm a sick old fart but yeah man, admit it — I like it — I like it! I am down here on the floor with one hell of a great big strong, young, muscle boy, right in front of me, that has got his enormous big, thick, stiff, black cock in my mouth, and I feel like I am on the top of the fucking world! Hell yes I like it — I love it — I never thought I'd ever be doing this, and hell yes — I love it! Oh, I wish I could see me right now! I wish I could see a picture of me eating the dick on this big beautiful man of a man, that has got his enormous rod stuck in my mouth! Oh shit man, that has got to look so fucking hot!"

"Wow man! What in the hell is happening down there man? What in the hell is happening! Holy shit man, what in the hell got into you all of a sudden? Jake, easy man, easy! Jake, take it slow! I mean man, that feels good, but don't kill yourself man, go slow! Whoa man, whoa!

All of a sudden, and without warning, Jake started in on Ken's dick like it was gonna fall off and roll away if he didn't go for it, and after it, as fast and as hard as he possibly could! All of a sudden, Jake fully accepted the basic fact that he did like having Ken's cock in his mouth, and he was all of a sudden fully determined to get every little bit of it into his mouth as much as possible! He grabbed ahold of Ken's butt muscles, squeezed each butt cheek with a good firm grip and attempted to pull Ken up and as close to his mouth as possible! He suddenly went from having only about two inches of Ken's cock into his mouth, to now having about four and a half or five inches of Ken's thick stiff rod into his mouth — and he was loving all of it! He couldn't breathe through his mouth, but he was liking it! All of a sudden he felt like his big muscled buddy had complete control over him, and he liked that feeling!

"Jake, Jake man! Slow down man, slow down! Jake, take it easy man, take it easy!"

Pulling off of Ken, and looking up at Ken's face, Jake quickly spurted out, "No! No man! I gotta take this and I wanna take it as fast as I can!"

Just as quickly as Jake had pulled off and told Ken how he wanted it all and he wanted it fast, he once again slammed him mouth back on to it, and went for it just as fast as possible. Ken stood there, offering his steak stick for all he could, and watched as his co-worker managed to ram his mouth onto his dick even farther than he had been earlier!

"Jake — Jake man! I've got about ten inches of fat dick man, don't try and take all of it right now! Save it man! Save some of it for later! Jake, Jake, gawd man, I've never had some guy go for it that damn fast, and especially his first time on it! Jake you're getting me awful close man! Gawd man, the way you're going for it man, you're getting it awful close man — it's getting real close man, it's getting real close! Jake, let me spray your chest man — let me spray your chest! Jake, I gotta cum man, I gotta cum!"

Realizing that Ken was actually pushing him back and was trying to pull his dick out of his mouth, Jake loosened up on his grip of not only Ken's dick but also Ken's torso and just as Ken managed to pull back ever so slightly, he watched as Ken's dick exploded in full force action as he let his dick full of cum fly out and spray warm creamy man cum, all over his chest!

"Oh shit man, oh shit! Oh Jake — oh gawd man — oh shit man, I shot like I was a fucking cannon or something! My gawd Jake, have you sucked off some guy before? Shit man — I sure as hell never expected you to get that fucking wild on me, man! Jake! What in the hell happened man, what in the hell happened? Shit man, I have never had some guy eat my dick like you just did! Jake, you OK? You OK?"

Still on his knees, down in front of the big six foot four, 234 pound, muscle bound, black man — the man with the ten inch long, and six inch around hard-on, pointing directly at his face, Jake looked up and after taking one deep breath, said, "Shit man! When that hit my chest, I thought the house had just been hit by a bomb! Shit man, what a fucking cum job you just shot at me! Shit man, it hit me like a shot from some big shotgun! Damn man, wow! Ken, my gawd man! Do all of you big black men shoot off that hard? I sure as hell know why you pushed me off of you before you let it all fly! Gawd man, that much cum shot down in my throat could have killed me with one hit! Wow man, I wanna watch you do that again! I gotta get more of my mouth on that thing next time! I gotta take all of it, I gotta!"

Gasping for air, attempting to regain his composure some, and grinning widely from ear to ear, Ken laughed and said, "Jake, look at your shirt! What a mess! Jake, I'm sorry! I'm sorry, but I had ta let it go, and there sure was no way in hell I was gonna take the time to take your shirt off of you before I let it fly! Hey guy, stand up here, we need to take that shirt off of you!"

Looking down at his shirt, Jake did reply, "Well, yeah, guess that is kinda of a big mess ain't it? My blue shirt looks more white now, than blue, don't it?"

"Ahhhhh — man. We kinda got us a little problem here man! I don't know if you've realized it yet or not, but that is a pull over T-shirt! Jake, you ready to have some of my cum spread all over your face? We pull that shirt up and off of you, you're gonna get a face full of dick juice! We can either do that, or ruin the shirt and cut if off of you — which you want?"

Looking at his shirt, then up at Ken, then back down to the mess on the front of his shirt, Jake said, "Well man — it's kinda like this! Yesterday at this time, I hadn't even watched two guys making it with each other yet, now today I've not only found out just how fucking great it is to get some big strong guy to suck me off and make my juices fly, but now I've even found out how fucking exciting it is to try and get more big thick stiff dick down in my mouth than I think I'll ever be able to do, so I guess maybe learning what a face full of cum feels like, is my next step."

"Tell you what Jake. I don't think it might be too smart for us to leave that shirt in the dirty clothes and have your wife find it and ask what it is — so why don't you take if off and I'll take it home with me and throw it in my wash. I can give it back to you at work, OK?"

"Hey guy, tell you what! Instead of you taking it home to wash it — how about we throw it in the wash here, along with the towels that we're gonna use after we shower each other down, and then get in the bedroom and have you teach me some more stuff about how two guys can make whoopee together, and give me another chance to see just how much of that tanker car of a dick you've got there, that I can get down into my throat! And, Ken, I will be real honest with you, now that we've done what we've done — last night on the web?"

"Yeah? Yeah what?"

"Ken when I typed in "black men", that was cause I really did want to see if I could find some pictures of a black man fucking the ass of some white guy. Yeah, I gotta be honest — when I found one, I started fantasying about that big black man, being you, and that little white guy under him, being me. Now that we've done this already, I'd kind of like to turn that fantasy into a reality! I'd really like for that big guy to be you, and the guy getting it in the ass, being me! Interested?"

"Oh shit man, you kidding? You want me to fuck your ass? Is that what you're saying?"

"Yeah, yeah I think so. I liked what I saw last night, and that's when I really got to thinking about you what you probably had for a dick. Course, now that I've seen it, I think it's a lot bigger than what maybe I expected, but yeah, yeah can you?"

"Hey man, if you're willing I sure as the hell am! Jake, I'm kinda really surprised that you wanna do that! I mean man, if you want to, of course

I do too, but since today is your first day doing this stuff, I was pretty sure that to even suggest that would scare the hell out of you and you'd say hell no! Yeah man, you're willing, I sure as the hell wanna do it!"

"Ken, it's OK if we try, ain't it? I wanna. Well, I think I want to anyway. Did you think I wouldn't want to cause of my ass or the size of your dick, or what? Why did you think that?"

"Hey man, I just didn't think you'd probably be that much game just yet. Most guys are usually kinda scared of getting it up the ass until they get a little more used to playing around and usually then only after they've fucked some other guy in the ass first, then they decide to try it. Course, once they do it, then they wonder just why they never did it before, and then they wanna do it all the time, but at first they're afraid. I'm game, I am. Of course I wanna fuck that butt, if you want me to!"

"Yeah Ken, yeah I do! Last night watching that stuff I found, I just couldn't stop thinking about it being you and me doing that, and I gotta admit, when I finally went to bed, I laid there with my fingers up in my ass trying to make believe it was you and your dick back there poking my ass. I know my fingers sure as hell are a lot smaller than that fucking dick you're carrying around, but Ken, seeing the size of that thing has just made me that much more anxious to see what it'd feel like up in there."

"OK guy, I sure do want to if you do. Wanna get that shirt off of you and then wash your face some before we get started?"

"Yeah, I do. Here help me pull if off of my head."

Jake and Ken each took ahold of the bottom of the shirt and pulled it up and finally over the top of Jake's head. Standin' back and laughing some, Ken said, "Well man, cum all over your face looks kinda good! How's it feel?"

"Funny, feels funny. I gotta see what it looks like in the mirror, then wash it off. Hey man, come on, let's take a shower and soap each other up some before we get started. OK?"

"Yeah, sure man. A shower sounds good to me! Let's do it."

Both men got themselves ready and after Jake managed to get the water temperature just bout right, both men stepped in and started wetting down.

"Oh Ken, this is great! Ken, I gotta admit, yesterday at this time I had no fucking idea at all that I'd find taking a shower with some guy so damn exciting, but just looking at you and that body you've got, it's all gotta be fun. Ken, you are one hot looking man! Built! Built like a fucking shit house! You used to play football in school, right?"

"Yeah, I did, but for some funny reason, I just wasn't as good as I should've been. Guess I was just more interested in watching the other guys, when the game was over and all of us were hitting the showers! Hey, never got to grab a guy's ass and his dick like this when I was with the football boys. Now I get to! How's that feeling?"

"Oh man, yeah, yeah! Keep it up Ken, keep it up! Shit man, never had somebody grab my dick and play with it like that before. Pull it, pull it!"

"Hey Jake, get me all soaped up. Get me all slippery and slimy. Yeah, oh yeah! Yeah, spread that all over me. Yeah, down under, get my ass all soapy! Soap me up man, soap me up!"

The space within the shower was not overly sized, especially considering Ken's 234 pounds of meat, and Jake's larger than average size of being about 195 pounds of beefy meat, himself.

"Hey Jake my man! You said you wrestled while in school right?"

"Yeah, but of course that's been some years ago now. Sure was fun though while I was doing it."

As Ken reached down and placed his right hand down and under Jake's crotch, he pulled up and asked, "So Mr. Wrestler Man, ever have some guy grab ahold of your dick like this? Ever have some guy play with you and your dick right out there on the mat, in front of the coach and the other guys?"

Standing there, letting the warm shower water fall across his face and chest, and also feeling the great feeling that Ken was offering by grabbing onto his dick and his bag, Jake replied with a very soft voice of admitting that, "Yeah, yeah! Ken, I remember those days with glee! I gotta admit, I really do not know, or understand, just why I never tried to play with some guy after those little sessions. I remember how excited I got when I felt their hands hit my dick or back by my ass! I guess I'd always been told that guys just were not supposed to do stuff with each other, so every time I thought about it, I convinced myself that I just wasn't supposed to do that stuff. Ken, last night, thinking about you, wondering just what you looked like all undressed, was just too much for me. I was eating supper, yeah—hot dogs, hot dogs and chips and when I put that hot dog on the bun, I got to wondering just how much bigger your dick probably was than that little hot dog. Ken, I guess I'm laying it all out. After looking at that dog, then I got to wondering about that sausage that's in the refrigerator. I took it out and handled it. I put it down by my crotch and then wondered if it was like your dick or was it bigger. That's when I got on the computer, just hoping I'd see some big long black dick, and then make believe one of 'em was yours. Ken, I'm serious, it wasn't until later today, about half an hour before we got off work, that I even thought about asking you to go get a beer. All of a sudden, I just could not stand it anymore, if I didn't talk to you and let you know what I looked at on the web. I saw so many guys and every time it was black guy, I wondered if his dick was like your dick!"

As Ken continued to rub and massage, Jake's ass and his crotch, he listened to Jake explain just what his previous day and night had been like, and then asked, "Jake — never ever played with any guy? You serious, never?"

"No, no Ken — never! Closest I ever did was one day at a roadside rest stop where some guy was taking a piss, and when he got done, he turned toward me, flipped his dick, about a nine of ten incher at me, and asked if I was interested. He told me he wanted to fuck my ass. Said he had a big rig truck outside where we could go, and do it. It was hard, and it made me hard! If I'd been all by myself, I'd have gone for it. That was the first time any guy ever asked me if I wanted to do something, and I couldn't! I wanted to, I did! When I told him I had to go, he reached over real quick, grabbed onto my crotch, and asked, 'You sure?' I had to get out of there, but I'll admit, I didn't want to. He knew I was hard. He squeezed it twice, and the second time, he squeezed hard!"

"Hey guy, when was that? How long ago's it been?"

"It's only been about two years ago. I was driving back from Illinois and of course Maryanne and the kids were with me, or I'd have done it. I would have done it that day! That guy was hot to me, he was hot! I would have loved to feel his dick up in my ass! I could have driven all the way home just knowing that I was sitting on an ass that had been fucked by one big strong man!"

Continuing to rub and play with Jake's bare, soap covered body, Ken asked, "What'd he look like? What kind of a guy was he?"

"Hey Ken, I'm not all hung up on black guys or anything, but yeah, he was a hot, hot, looking black guy! Looked like he was probably about 30 years old, looked like he could have been a cop. You know how cops look! For some reason, they just look hot, regardless of if they have their uniform on or not. I really do think that's why he reached out and grabbed me. He wanted me to know he wasn't some cop. Damn man, I wish I could have played with him. I kept thinking about him and the way he came onto me a lot. Then — about only six months later, you came to work. Ken, you do not know how many times I have compared you to him. Every day I've looked at that bulge in your crotch and wondered if your dick was as hot looking as that guy's was. There have been days when I swore you two were brothers. You two look a lot alike. Now that I've seen it, I can honestly tell you, you sure as hell are hung bigger and longer than he was, but his was still nice! I've wondered ever since that day, just what his dick slammed up in my ass could have felt like. Ken, that's why I'm so anxious to have you fuck me. I've been wanting it ever since that day, two years ago, out in a roadside rest area. I wish he could have followed us all the way home! I'd loved to have found him later sometime."

Looking down at Jake, slightly letting his lips touch the back of Jake's neck, Ken softly said, "You'll get it — you're gonna get it! It got hard all over again listening to you telling me about your roadside buddy, and it's ready to take care of you. It ain't gonna be his dick, but it is gonna be mine, and I'm gonna make sure you enjoy it as if it was his, in his big rig truck! Come on man, let's get all rinsed off and get in bed. I'm hard, ready and anxious to see just how fast and how far you can take this little piece of meat I got to feed you!"

"Ken my man, that ain't no small piece of meat man — no small piece of meat. Ken, I wanna do this, but please go slow and easy on me, please! I've never had anything bigger than my finger up in my ass before, we need to go slow! I know guys can take big dicks up in their butts, and I've heard about guys getting fists stuck up in there, so I know it can be done, but please be easy on me till I get it in me, OK? I know it's gonna be hurting me some, I know it's gotta! But man, I've heard it's great and now you're the only one that knows I want to do it. God, your cock is so fucking big, I hope like hell I can take it OK! I just hope I can!"

Still standing in the shower, the warm water still softly flowing down across their bodies, Jake could tell that Ken had stooped down just far enough to slide his hot, stiff, boner up between his legs, and was now sliding it back and forth, up against his ass creek and crevice! He could feel the length of it, the warmth of it, and the strength of it up against his ass. He pushed his ass back toward Ken, to let Ken know that his ass was hot and hungry! He was definitely enjoying the feel of it sliding in and out of his ass crevice, and he was definitely looking forward to feeling it slide back and forth, in and out, of his ass!

Both men grabbed a towel and dried off, and Ken then told Jake that he was gonna put on enough clothes to run out to his car and get a tube of lube out of his gym bag. "I'll be right back in, but I do think maybe we'd better pack that tight little butt of your with some KY and get some on my dick! I want you to take this dick with out screaming, and so I really do think maybe we need to get some lube for it. I'll be right back!"

Ken came back in, lube in hand, and filled Jake's rear end with a lot of lube! "Jake my man, trust me man, you're gonna take it! Your ass is begging for it, it's begging! Lay down on that bed man, spread those legs, open that ass, get ready! I've got one big boner that needs to feel the inside of that ass! Lay still man, we're gonna do this, and you're gonna be fucking glad we did! You're gonna think you've finally got your trucker man, and he's finally got your ass! You ready man? Ready? I'm gonna start by kissing your ass and licking your ass and getting it all hot and ready! First you're gonna feel my tongue run up in there and then after it's all good and slick, then my little boner is gonna creep up in there and take all of it! It's gonna do your ass! It's gonna go in just as deep as it can go! You're gonna feel it up in your gut! Here I come man, here I come! Face, fingers, tongue and then my dick! My big black boner of a dick! You're gonna get fucked, gonna get fucked for the first time, and you're gonna get fucked big time — with a big one! You're gonna remember this for the rest of your life! Lay still, relax, and open that sweet ass of yours! We are gonna become a hell of a lot closer than just two co-workers man — one hell of a lot closer!"

I Am Really, Really, Ready!

Chapter One: Joe and Troup's Walk

For about four months now, Joe has been taking his German Shepherd dog for an early morning walk around his neighborhood. The earliest that he usually heads out is about 6:30 and the latest is about 7:15. He usually takes the same route around the neighborhood, and it's only the time element that usually varies.

Joe is a young, blond haired, well built, married man, just turned 25 years old, was a former wrestler in high school, and now works as a truck driver for a delivery firm.

Realizing that sitting behind the wheel of a truck is not the greatest way to stay in good physical shape, Joe does visit his local gym at least 3 or 4 times a week for a good work-out. It's working, he still looks like a very young strong and muscled wrestler.

Lately Joe has noticed some rather peculiar circumstances at one house along his morning walks.

A very nice and very neatly kept older Victorian Style house over on Miller Street was creating some curiosity for him. Well, not exactly the house, but rather some of the activity that he "thinks" is going on at that house.

About a month ago, Joe noticed a person watching him from the front window. No problem! He figured anybody has the right to look out of their front window. He attempted to not be noticed. He did not want anybody to know that he could see them.

On the following day, the same thing happened, and once again Joe did not feel like there was any reason to even be aware of it. Their house, they can look out if they want to.

Knowing that he was probably being watched as he walked by, Joe did attempt to keep from looking at that house when he was close by. That did work, he assumed since it had been a few days since he had last noticed anybody looking out of that house.

Then things changed.

When he first saw that person, he could see only the upper part of his torso, as if he was sitting in a chair. Joe could tell that it was a man, but could not see him well enough to know really what he looked like or what age he might be. The one very obvious thing that he could tell, and it would be pretty hard to miss — the man was a black man.

Now, on this day, that person was standing up, but not close to the window. The person was visible, but obviously was back in the room some. Joe did not make any indication that he had seen that person. He casually continued his walk, although if his dog, Troup, wanted to stop and smell something in that area, Joe did not rush him as much as he might have before this mysterious person had come to his attention. In-fact, for Troup to decide right then to stop for a moment, was a convenience to Joe since it did give him the opportunity to just stand there and of course casually look around.

As the days continued, the mysterious man would always seem to be there, regardless of what time Joe and Troup walked by. Joe could only imagine that, that gentlemen did not have a very strict time schedule that he had to live by. He was always there and looking out at Joe, regardless of how early or how late he happened to be.

In curiosity, Joe was starting to find this a rather interesting situation, and Joe started to wonder just how flexible this man's schedule was, so he changed his route and showed up in front of that house much earlier than usual.

Seeing the man watching him, very early, Joe then changed his route the next day so that he would be going past the house quite late. The man was there, and the man was watching.

It was now obvious to Joe, that regardless of what time he and Troup walked by, that man was there and was watching.

Once again Joe thought, well so be it! It's his house. He can do as he pleases!

A week or so went by and Joe daily expected to see his unknown admirer, and he was not disappointed. The man was there each day, standing back away from the window, but none the less watching.

Troup did seem to give Joe more opportunities to stop in front of that house than he did originally, in-fact Troup stopped and sniffed the ground right in front of that house every day now. Joe wondered if Troup could tell that he was not in such of a hurry once they got onto that street.

Suddenly after quite a number of days all being the same, Joe noticed that one small item had now changed. His admirer apparently had not had sufficient time to get fully dressed. On this particular morning he was wearing only his white briefs, and the contrast between the white cotton and the man's dark skin was very obvious.

Joe thought, "Oh! If he knows that I have been able to see him, then he has to know I can see him today, too!"

Joe made no actions that indicated he even knew the man was there. During this entire time of first seeing him close to the window, clear up to this day, Joe had never given any indication that he was aware of the man.

The following day, the same attire, or lack of, if you prefer that reference, the following day, the same and this did continue for six days. Joe noticed, but never reacted. He simply let Troup spend whatever time he needed out by the sidewalk, and then they would move on.

Up until the first day of seeing the man with nothing on except the white briefs, Joe had not really thought too much about what he was aware of, and he did not mention it to his wife, Sharon, since it was really no big deal. But now that things had changed slightly, he has glad that he had not mentioned it to her, since he was not too sure of just what was going on, and he was glad he did not have to try and explain anything to anybody.

Joe really did feel now, that he actually was, much more of a specific interest to the man in the house, than just a person that walked his dog down the street every morning.

Until the white briefs showed up, Joe had actually thought that maybe, just maybe this man was always there and watching out his front window, although he did wonder just why he had moved back into the center of the room somewhat.

On the sixth day, Joe at first thought that his admirer was not in the room. He did not see him.

As Joe realized that the man was actually in there, Joe was concerned that he could have been too obvious when looking toward the house.

The man was there, but the reason Joe did not see him was — no white briefs! Just and only, dark mahogany skin! The very bright white briefs had been a main stay for almost a week now, and now all of a sudden, they were nowhere in sight!

Joe could only hope that he had not been obvious in looking toward the house, and more so, was hoping that when he realized that the man was actually standing there, that his facial expression did not change too dramatically. Joe did not know for sure if the gentlemen inside did, or did not know that Joe could see him.

Joe thought, "Well, maybe he does think that the reflection on the glass keeps me from being able to see him, and maybe that is the reason why he moved back from sitting too close!"

The following morning, Joe was rather anxious to take his walk down Miller Street. This situation was becoming intriguing to him. He had the mystery in his mind about if this man did, or did not know he could be seen.

As Joe approached the front of the house, Troup again, as was now becoming very normal, stopped and wanted to spend quite an amount of time sniffing along the edge of the yard.

Attempting to be very nonchalant about it, Joe did, more so now than on any other day, look at the house to see if the man was there.

Joe looked up. Yes! He was there, and somewhat closer to the window than before, and showing only the mahogany skin. No briefs!

Joe tried to act as if he could not see anything, but he was getting way too sure that the man knew, just plain simply knew, that Joe could see him.

As Joe and Troup were out front, the man stood as if a statue. He did not move at all. He stood solid, which was a term that Joe had already put in conjunction with the man. Solid!

Joe had noticed, although he was actually trying not to, he had noticed that the man looked very, very, solid. Joe knew that since there were no briefs, that there should have been, or actually had been a dick for him to see, but in his embarrassed manner of realizing some other man was now displaying himself to him, he had not even looked at it. Joe had never been in a situation like this before, where it was now obvious that some other guy was wanting Joe to see him, and the — all of him!

In his wrestling days he certainly did have his opportunities to be completely naked and bare in front of a lot of guys, and them, naked and bare in front of him, but he had never experienced a time when a man was almost putting a sign around his neck that read, "I'm naked-look at me!"

In one way, Joe was kind of shook that something this weird was happening to him, but then at the same time, he was kind of glad that some guy apparently thought well enough of him, that he wanted to display his complete body in front of him.

Joe called to Troup and moved on. His experience was confusing to him. He did not know how he was actually supposed to react.

Was he to be mad? Mad that some guy would stand there all naked, and want him, or expect him to look at him?

The following day, quite rather the same experience, except—the man was now closer to the front window. Once again, standing as if a statue, but none-the-less, standing there showing everything!

One more day, one more step closer to the window.

One more day, one more step closer to the window.

One more day, one more step closer to the window.

Five days total, and the man was almost within touching distance of the window.

As Joe saw him so close to the front of the room, and now actually in a very obvious view, he turned and looked to see if there were any others on the street that could possibly see the naked man too. Joe did not see anybody, and then he realized that if there had been, the man in the window would have already seen them.

Joe looked at the man, and looked directly at his eyes.

The man was looking back directly into Joe's eyes too.

Joe was somewhat, kind of, in a state of shock and he simple stood there and looked at the man. There was some glare reflection coming back from the glass, but it was now very, very obvious that the man inside knew Joe could see him, and all of him.

Suddenly Joe turned, called for Troup to follow, and he headed down the street.

The following morning, Joe actually fought with himself about if he should even go down Miller Street, or if he needed to change his morning route. He knew he should avoid that street, so that he was no longer confronted with the weird — way too weird of a situation, that had been going on for a long time now.

But — his curiosity of wanting to see what could now happen — won!

Joe and Troup started down Miller Street.

They approached the front of their mystery house.

Much to Joe's surprise, the man was not in view in the window, and for the very first morning for a long time, Troup did not seem to have a strong interest in sniffing the grass as he had been doing for quite some time.

Joe, although shocked that he did not have the naked man to see, continued on down Miller Street.

Softly, and to him very suddenly, he heard someone lowly yell out, "Joe, hey Joe, come over here!"

Joe stopped, and looked around.

"Hey Joe, come over here, in front of the blue Buick." The unseen person again said.

Joe turned and realized that beside his rather mysterious house, in a very vine covered, trellis type of a carport, was a blue Buick.

Joe turned, looked up and down the street. He turned toward the car and paused. He felt like he should run, and he also was way too curious to even want to think about leaving this place without finding out just what in the hell was going on.

He thought, "I've got Troup with me! For God's sake, nobody in their right mind would do anything to me, with me having my 90 pound German Shepherd with me!"

He started so very slowly toward the car.

"Yeah, thanks Joe." The voice said.

"God, he knows my name! What in the hell is going on here? Who in the hell is it that knows my name?" He thought to himself.

He continued to approach the car.

"Joe, I'm over here in front of the car, behind some of the vines. You're OK, everything's OK. Just come on around the front of the car.

Joe cautiously continued his walk toward the front of the car, and then went past the front of the car, and could see where the man was standing. And he could also see that he was outside — completely naked, and showing every square inch of his black skin — from head to toe!

Joe froze! He did not know what to do. Troup stood beside him, and was actually wagging his tail some! Joe did not know if to stand there, or if to turn and run as fast as he could.

"Joe, it's Coach Wilson from over at East Side High."

Joe kind of leaned forward and said, "What!? What did you say?"

"Joe, everything is OK. I'm Coach Wilson from over at East Side High. You know who I am. You're okay! Joe, I want to talk to you! Can we talk?"

As Joe kind of tried to say, "Okay, yeah I guess", he noticed that Troup was eating something from on the ground. It looked like a piece of bread and butter.

Joe looked at Troup, was quite shocked that his dog was more interested in that piece of bread than in what was going on, and he looked at Coach Wilson.

And yeah — when he looked at Coach Wilson, he truly did have something to look at! He had never had such an opportunity to, so completely, look over a completely bare and naked, mature, and very, very muscular, man. Including his hard-on!

Joe was feeling very shocked and confused. Coach Wilson was, in his mind, the hottest looking wresting coach, of any team he had competed against, during his wrestling days. Coach Wilson was really very well built, was now in his mid forty's and stood about 6' 3 or 4. Joe had always thought of him as one damn hot, and damn good looking man!

"Coach Wilson. Coach of the wrestling guys over at East High? You were the coach over there when I competed against the East Side High guys, weren't you?"

"Yeah Joe, I was. Joe, even back then, I wanted to get my hands on your body and play with it, but of course I was a coach and you were a student, so I had to stay in line. But Joe, I admired you back then, and I have never forgotten about you! So when I first saw you walking your dog down our street, I just knew I had to see if maybe, just maybe, I could have another chance at you."

"Joe, I know you're married. I've been kind of keeping track of you. I know you work for City and County Delivery."

"Joe, your Senior year, when you took county First Place from my wrestler, I really was happy as hell, although I couldn't show it. My God! Can you image the scandal it would have created if it ever got known that I was cheering for you over my own student! Joe when you won, I wanted to run out on the middle of the floor and give you a big hug and a kiss. Joe, you have had me all hot and bothered ever since the first time that I saw you when you were a Freshman!"

"I've even gotten the school to switch over to using City and County Delivery whenever we need something picked up or delivered, just in the hope that you would be the driver."

"Joe, when I saw you walking the dog down our street, I decided I just had to find out if maybe you might be agreeable to having sex with me. Joe, you've been watching me for weeks now as I kept getting more and more brazen is showing my body to you, and you kept looking, so I finally decided I needed to let you know what I want. Joe, will you let me suck you off?"

"Coach, I can't do that! Coach, I'm married. I'm married to a women, I'm not gay!"

"Hey Joe, I'm married too, and I'm not really gay, but once in awhile when I can find me a really hot one, then I like to do some—like extra—type of stuff. And Joe, I have thought you are a really hot one for way too long now. Joe, please don't turn me down! I've wanted this for years, now. Joe, I want you and me to do it, man!"

"Joe, I'm married too. My wife is a nurse at City Hospital and she works from about 6:00 in the morning, and that's why I've been able to kind of play around with you, trying to find out if you might be approachable. Joe, let me tell you something man. You are approachable, or you would have changed your walking habits away from this house weeks ago. You may not know it, but as things kept getting more and more "funny", the more you got all excited about it. And you did, didn't you?"

"Yeah! God yes, I guess I do have to admit so, coach! Like this morning, I tried to tell myself that after what happened yesterday, seeing you completely naked in your front window, I tried to convince myself that I needed to go someplace else, but then I just had to come by here to see if I would see you all naked again. Man, you've got nerve standing there all naked in your window like that!"

"No — not really Joe. I could see everything outside. I knew it was just you and your dog. Oh — and by the way, Joe. Don't you think it is kind of funny that your dog got to where he wanted to spend a lot of time in front of my house? He was getting some butter treat that I was putting out there on the grass each morning, so that he'd want to stop and sniff and lick. That gave me more of a chance to watch you and dream about you and me getting together. And it gave me more time to see if you would turn and run when I started showing myself to you. You never did, did you? In-fact, here you are today, after I showed you, through my front window, the big black meat stick that you could chew on. You're back, so I guess you kind of accepted my invitation, didn't you?"

"Oh God Coach! Shit man! You have got me so damn confused right now! Man, I never thought about playing around with some guy, but shit man, then I never thought that it might be somebody like you. Yeah, coach, I'm getting awfully close to saying yes to you, but it's just because it's you. If you were some other guy, I'd tell him hell no, but Coach, I remember back in the high school days, and I was always anxious to wrestle your guys — because I knew you would be there. So I kind of guess, even back then, I must've been kind of attracted to you, even though I didn't realize it. Right?"

"Yeah, Joe. I think you were, but you just didn't know it. You got me all hot and bothered at one match we had with your team because I caught you looking at me once, and I almost melted on the damn floor. Joe, I've never made it with any of the school guys, but there have been some times, when I was sucking on some other guy's cock, and I made believe to myself, that it was you! Joe, you can not imagine how many times I have imagined that I had your dick in my mouth when, in reality, it was some other guy's dick."

"Hey coach — you know — I never thought about it, but now I kind of remember how really excited I always got, when I got to be around you. Do you think I was kind of hot for you back then, and I just didn't know what I was feeling? Coach, I did not know this was your place, but do you think that since I could kind of see you in the front window, and even though I didn't know it was you, I could tell it was somebody that was pretty close to being like you, and that's why I was so interested? Do you think that I was unconsciously hoping, in the back of my mind, that it might be you? Coach, do you think that is possible?"

"Coach, do you think that maybe you are the real reason that I have always kind of watched big muscular black men, when I happened to be around them? Coach do you think that maybe I have really had this deep down inside thing for you all of this time, and I just never figured it out? Coach, yeah, hell yes, I do want to have some sex with you! It sure did take me a few minutes to figure myself out, but God I'm glad we could talk!" "Coach, really within just these last few minutes, I do think I understand me, a lot better. Coach, I never thought that I wanted gay sex, but oh my God! Coach, just all of a sudden, I am hotter for having sex than I have ever been before!"

"Coach, I never realized that I wanted to have sex with another guy, but shit man, right now I am so damn excited and anxious and I am really — really, ready! Shit coach, I didn't feel this way just a few minutes ago. Coach, I am ready! Oh coach! I am so damn horny all of a sudden! You will have to teach me, man! I've never had sex with a guy before! Oh man! Oh my God man, just look at the size of that dick on you! Shit man, I did not know a guy could have a rod that fucking big! Oh Coach, all of a sudden, I can't believe me man, I can't. Just a few minutes ago, I had no idea that I even wanted to look at some other guy's dick — but my God Man — look at what in the hell you are hanging there! It is a fucking telephone pole, it is! Oh, Coach, can I grab your dick? Oh God man! Let's do it, please! Oh Coach! Let's do it before I realize what I am doing and I try to change my mind!"

Chapter Two: One was a Real Muscular Black Guy

"Joe, your dog can stay here in the back yard. It's fully enclosed and he can't get out. Come with me. I'm so excited and happy that I will finally get to do what I have dreamt of doing for years. Joe, I am sure you are gonna to be real glad that we got together, and we're with each other." Coach told Joe, as he opened the gate into the backyard, and invited the hunky young man in.

"Coach, like I said, we had better get started on this right away or I might change my mind. I'm still not sure I should be doing this! Is Troup going to be okay here in the yard for a while?"

"Yeah, Joe. Troup's going to be okay out here. Come here young man. I want to put by arms around you like I have wanted to do for years now." Coach Wilson took Joe by the shoulders and pulled him up close and tight.

"Oh Coach! Coach I'm not going to say I don't want to do this, but man, I'm feeling real nervous right now. Coach, I never expected something like this to happen man!" Joe returned the hug. He slowly put his hands around the coach's waist and hugged.

"Oh Coach! You do feel good to me! You feel so strong, man! Coach, we had better get inside or I'm still afraid that I will want to change my mind, but I've got to admit that having your arms around me, and mine around you, is really making me feel like I'm not really doing anything wrong here. Coach, hug me tight and then let's get inside so I can get undressed."

"Yeah, OK Joe. We can do that, but if you have not noticed, I'm completely bare assed naked out here, and if you want, you can get naked out here too. This back yard is completely closed in and nobody can see us in here, well—unless an airplane flies over, so if you want we can go in the house, or we can stay out here."

"Oh coach. Yeah, yeah! Let's stay out here then if we can. I've never played outside before, well if you know what I mean, like have sex. Oh yeah! That sounds like fun!"

With that comment, Joe let loose of the coach, and the coach moved his hands down to start removing Joe's warm-up slacks. Joe looked down, watched the coach take ahold of the top snap and let out a big breath.

"Getting all nervous with me starting to take off your pants?" The coach asked.

"Yeah, I guess I must be." Replied Joe. "Coach, you've got to admit that a hell of a lot of stuff is going through my mind right now. Years ago I know I could of almost begged you to do this, and hell back then, I never in the greatest of imagination could I have ever thought that the day would come where you are taking my pants off of me. And Coach — look at that mammoth cock of yours! Shit it is big! Coach, for God's sake, Coach! You aren't expecting to do anything with that damn big thing are you? I mean, you're not wanting to put that up in my ass or anything are you? Coach, please tell me that you're not wanting to try and fuck me with that damn big thing, are you? Coach, you know my ass could never get that big thing up in there! Please coach, please let me know that all you want to do is maybe suck on me! Please! Really, if you think that maybe you want to try and get that think up inside of me, I'm going to run. Coach that damn pole would rip a guy's ass all apart. I'm serious coach, tell me if you are planning on trying to use my ass!"

"No, no Joe! No, I will not try to put that rod up in your ass. Today, all I want to do is get a good long chance to finally put your dick in my mouth and suck some juices out of it, and if you want to lick on my pole some, then of course I'll let you do that. But if you don't want to, then that's OK too. Joe I'm not going to make you do anything that you do not want to do."

"Thanks Coach! Thanks! Seriously Coach, that rod is bigger than any guy's dick I've even seen pictures of. Is that natural? I mean, you didn't have some way to get it enlarged did you?"

"No Joe, it's all natural. I guess I just happened to be in the right line the day I was given a dick before I was born. Somebody up there must have decided that I needed a little more than the usual, so I've had this thing ever since I grew up."

"Coach, does your wife take it OK? Can you screw her OK? I mean, I don't mean to be getting real personal here about you and your wife, but shit man, can she take that thing?"

Coach looked at Joe, and with a grin on his face told Joe, "Yeah man she loves it. Whenever she gets mad at me, she tells me that she would leave me, except she don't want to leave my dick behind. So she says she will put up with me, just so she don't have to let my dick go! I may piss her off once in awhile, but my dick is a lifesaver for me!"

Joe reached down and as he grinned about the coach's statement, he put his hand on it.

"Oh my God Coach! Coach, I can't close my hand around it! Coach, my God man! How big is that? Have you ever measured it, I mean, do you have anyway of knowing how big around that thing is?"

"Yeah, Joe. I measured it once. I got asked by so many others how big it was, that I got tired of telling 'em that I didn't know, so one day I did measure it, when it was good and hard. On that day, when I measured it, it was just about nine and a half inches around, and from my body out to the tip of it, it was nine and a half inches. So I've always kind of just joked that I have a square dick, since it measures nine and a half by nine and a half."

"Oh my God Coach! Have you ever tried to put that thing up in a guy's ass before? I mean, man, is there any guy that could take that much rod up in his ass without tearing it all apart?"

"Yeah, Joe. Yeah! I've fucked a few guys before. Some that I really was not interested in, but those were the guys that had heard about it, and they really insisted that I fuck their ass just so they could say that they had taken it before. And, got to tell you, everyone of them took it, and some of them took it real fast!"

With that comment, the coach continued to undo Joe's warm-ups and he slightly moved them down onto his hips. He grabbed the bottom of Joe's pull over shirt, and pulled it up and off of his head. As he let loose of the shirt with his left hand, he brought it down and placed in on the shoulder blade of Joe's back. He lowered his right hand, dropped the shirt on the ground and grabbed Joe's ass cheek. He lowered his head down, and placed his lips on Joe's right nipple. The coach sucked on that tit, and then took the tip of it in his mouth and slightly bit. Joe groaned a very pleasant groan of satisfaction and pleasure. Coach moved his mouth to the left nipple and again sucked and bit. Joe again released a pleasant moan and an encouraging groan. The coach knew that he had found some of Joe's sexually sensitive spots. He pulled Joe up close and tight. He hugged Joe, and Joe hugged back.

The coach then slipped his thumbs into the top of Joe's' warm-up pants and pulled them on down to his knees.

"Well — look at that!" The coach exclaimed! "Damn Joe, that looks hot! Damn man! Got to admit, those are a surprise to me, I figured that you would just have on some boring ole white briefs, but shit man, you know how to dress. Joe, those shorts are damn hot on you! Shit man, look at the basket they show! I know they're under shorts, but shit man, I think it would be a benefit to the entire neighborhood if you just wore those and no pants on top of 'em! Shit man, those are hot!"

Joe was wearing a longer and more form fitting pair of undershorts that definitely hugged his body tight, and with the pronounced, crotch basket insert of the shorts, it really showed off all of Joe's assets. The insert became a complete package and display all of its own, the way it was cut and designed to show off every possible part of a guy's crotch that he had available.

"Joe, do you wear this type of shorts every day?"

"Uh no!" Joe replied. "No, I really don't! Today is the first time that I have worn them while out walking Troup. Coach, I guess, thinking back on it, I kind of guess that maybe without me actually realizing it, seeing you in the window like I have lately must have gotten me somewhat excited, although I didn't know it. The other day, I was downtown in the mall, and all of a sudden I wanted something more exciting to wear than just the normal usual stuff, and so when I saw these, they just looked kind of exciting to me, and so I bought 'em. Today's the first day I've worn them, and I guess maybe that's because without knowing it, I was getting all sexy feeling with the stuff that has been going on here. Do you think I was unconsciously hoping that something like this would happen today?"

"You know Joe, you might have. We as humans do some weird things sometimes that we never realize. Maybe the last few days of seeing me in the window has gotten you kind of excited, but you never wanted to admit it to yourself."

As the coach was finishing his statement, and his admiration of the hot looking under shorts, he pulled them on down and let Joe's cock and bag jump out of confinement.

"Yeah, yeah! I thought so!" Coach exclaimed. "Yeah, I thought so!"

"You thought so what? What?" Joe questioned as he looked at the coach with a very quizzed look on his face.

"Joe, ever since your high school days and the wrestling matches, I had just been sure you were really nicely hung for a white guy! Yeah — Joe! You are! Look at that rod and those balls you're carrying around. Yeah, yours might not be as big as mine, that I will agree, but shit man, have you ever compared your dick to some other white guys' dicks? Joe, you are well hung! Nicely, very, well hung!"

"Well coach, I've never really ever compared it, but yeah there have been times when some other guys that saw it made comments about it. I never really thought it was any different than others though. Is it really that much bigger than other white dicks?"

"Yeah Joe, it is. You know man, ever since your wrestling days I was just damn sure you were carrying more in that wrestling singlet of yours than other guys. Every time you wrestled against my boys, I had my eyes on that crotch almost all of the time. You know Joe. For years now I have been afraid that I would never get the chance to see for myself if you really were carrying more than usual. I guess your coaches never suggested to you that when you get dressed that maybe you might want to tuck that big rod down under your crotch so it doesn't show so much, uh?"

"Well no, nobody ever told me I was showing too much. God Coach! Coach, do you think maybe my own coaches were letting me do that just so they could look at it too? Do you think that is possible?"

"Well Joe. You always showered after a wrestling match, right?"

"Yeah, of course I did."

"Well, just tell me how often your coach would just happen to be in the shower room when you just happened to be showering. Very often?"

"Yeah Coach. Yeah! Always! Coach — Coach Bradley, my first coach and then Coach Snyder, the one I had my Senior year, they were always in the shower room when I was in there. Are you saying that they were there just to see how I was hung? That is the reason they were there? Not to do the stuff they acted like they were doing, but just to see me naked?"

"Yeah Joe, I think so! Joe, I don't need to be in the shower room with my guys after a match, unless — that is — unless — I've got some hot hung wrestler that I want to check out. Sure, then I'll find a reason to be in there, but not normally. Joe my dear man! You were being checked out by your coaches and probably all of the other wrestlers too. I will tell you one thing man. I did notice that every time my guys wrestled you, well in fact every time I ever saw any guy wrestle you, you always got grabbed in the crotch area a hell of a lot

115

more than the normal wrestler. I kind of figured, for the entire time that I knew you back then, that a lot of high school wrestlers were getting a lot of good chances to do a lot of crotch grabbing on you. A lot of high school wrestlers in this area have felt that dick and bag of balls. A lot of wrestlers in this area know just how your dick and your balls feel, I know that for sure! I know I'm one coach that always wanted to have the chance to do some grabbing down there on you too! You have probably been felt up more than any other guy in this area. Didn't you ever have the feeling that some of those guys were doing a whole lot more grabbing and feeling, down in that area, than what was probably necessary? Hell Joe, I'm sure a lot of those guys could have wrestled better if they had been concentrating on their wrestling instead of trying to feel you up. Hell, some of my own wrestlers probably lost some of their matches with you since they were probably more interested in knowing what you were hung like, and what you felt like, instead of knowing what winning felt like! I watched some of their faces pretty closely when they were wrestling you, and I saw a lot of guys' faces, that unconsciously lit up, when they grabbed your basket. They grabbed it on purpose. They didn't realize that some of us had caught on and were watching to see how often you got grabbed down there. The hell with wrestling — they were on that mat to feel you and your crotch, and damn near every one of them did! They just didn't realize that the entire gymnasium full of people, were watching them feel you up! And of course some of them were their Moms and Dads!"

Coach Wilson then took ahold of Joe's manly equipment and uttered, "Wow! Shit man! I've never seen a white guy with that much between his legs! Well, you were wondering just a few minutes ago of how big I was, and I can see that before too long we will be using the ole tape measure on you." And with that statement, Coach bent down, took ahold of Joe's cock and placed it in his mouth.

Joe, still not completely comfortable that they were having sex outdoor, in the backyard, again looked around to make sure that nobody could see what was happening in the coach's backyard. "Nobody can see in here, right, Coach?"

Pulling Joe's body up closer to himself so that he could take the entire white rod down his throat, the coach answered the best that he could, "No, nobody can see. Hey fuck my mouth, you white stud!"

Joe regained his attention back to the sucking that he was getting. He watched the coach suck on his dick, and started forgetting about them being outside, and started getting "into" the sucking that was happening!

"Oh man!" Joe exclaimed with gusto. "Oh man that feels good! Oh Coach, that feels really good! Yeah man, that is great. Oh Coach this is great!"

Joe grabbed the coach's head and pulled it toward himself!

"Oh Coach, I've never had a suck off before! Of Coach, I did not know they felt this good! Oh Coach, suck on it!"

The coach pulled off for a moment and replied, "I am man, and I am finally getting what I have wanted for years! Oh Joe you taste so good to me!"

The coach immediately went back on Joe's dick and grabbed Joe's ass muscles to force Joe's dick as far into his mouth as possible! Joe was getting excited and was giving the coach as much cock as he had to offer.

"Oh Coach, chew on it! Coach let me know that you have got me and my dick in your mouth! Oh Coach, suck me please!"

The coach had Joe's meat rod in his mouth, and he was using it to his complete joy, He had ahold of Joe's backside and steadied Joe's body as he forced his face on to and off of Joe's man stick meat. Faster and faster he went onto and off of Joe's cock! He was sucking him furiously, manly and wildly! Coach Wilson was finally getting the stick of meat that he had dreamt of for years now, and he was using it for all he could do!

Oh Coach! Coach, I think I'm getting read to cum man! Coach, I'm going to cum! Coach, I gonna cumm man — oh Coach — Coach! I'm cummmin!! I'm cummmmin Coach! Oh shit man! I just shot a big wad of my cum, all of my cum, in your mouth Coach! Coach, was I supposed to do that, Coach?"

As he could recompose himself, Coach continued to swallow Joe's cum, lick the sides of Joe's dick, and continued to suck with force to make sure that he had taken all of the young man juices and he then said, "Hell yes Joe! Hell yes, you were supposed to feed me your cum! Hell yes man! That is what you were supposed to do and exactly what I wanted! Yeah man, yeah — you did good! Oh Joe, I knew for years a rod like that one had to be a good rod to suck on! Oh Joe, what a fucking rod of meat you've got man! Joe, please promise me that I will be able to do you again real soon!"

"Coach, Coach, I want you to try and fuck me! Coach please, I want to see if you can fuck me! Will you Coach?"

Coach Wilson immediately bounced back off of Joe's dick, looked up at Joe and quickly asked, "What!? Joe you want what? Joe you said you want me to fuck you? You mean in your ass? Joe, is that what you asked!?"

"Yeah Coach — yeah that's what I said. Will you see if I can take it? I know I'm probably out of my fucking mind, but Coach — I really do wanna see if I can get it up in my butt! Please!"

"Hell yes Joe, I sure will, but my God man — what in the hell made you decide that we could do that? Joe I wasn't even sure that I was going to get to just suck on your cock, and now you are asking me to try and fuck your ass? Joe are you sure? Joe do you know what you are asking?"

Coach, I got it in the butt once by a bunch of guys, and ever since then I've been real confused about what I want to do or how I feel about stuff. It really hurt that day, but I think I want to try it again, but I was afraid to say so. Right now I just decided that I needed to tell you what I want."

"Coach, I almost turned those guys into the police that day, and then I didn't and ever since then I've wondered why I didn't. Coach, I think if I get fucked again, even by a really big, fucking big one like yours, then maybe I can forget all about that day. Will you?"

"Yeah, I will Joe, but tell me what happened. What happened and when was that? What in the hell happened to you?"

Coach I had just turned 18, and it was after a baseball game over at Wood Park. We played a team from over in Collier County, and a bunch of their guys cornered me in the restroom after the game and they all fucked me. It hurt Coach, it hurt! None of them tried to use anything on my ass. They all fucked me dry and it really hurt! I found out later that when a guy gets fucked in the ass, that he uses some grease or something in his ass, and they didn't do that to me. When they came in the restroom, one of them said something like, "Hey man. We hear from your buddies that you have got one hell of a big cock and you like to play with guys!" Then all of a sudden two of them had ahold of me, they pushed me up against the wall, and the other one pulled my pants down. They all grabbed my dick and pulled on it and slapped it back and forth. Yeah — coach — they made it get hard and when it did then they all said, "Yeah man! He's a gay faggot! He's a faggot!"

Then they turned me around to face the wall and each one of them fucked my ass. I heard one of them tell me something about since they weren't faggots they weren't going to suck on my dick, but they sure didn't have any problem fucking my cute little ass! That's when two of them would hold me and then the other one would fuck me. I was mad and after they finally left I really did want to call the cops, but then I was afraid that when people heard about what happened, then everybody would think I was a faggot, so I just never called them."

"Well, what happened to those guys? Who were they? Weren't they on the team bus? How did they have this much time?"

All I know about them was that two of them were on the team, and I guess it was the third guy that was older, and he had a car. One of them was kind of a small guy, but his fucking dick felt big, one was a real muscular black guy, with of course a big dick, and with no grease up in my ass, I'm sure it felt bigger than it really was, and then the third guy was the older one. He looked like a biker to me. He wore a lot of leather and silver stuff. I remember he had really big boots on! Funny thing was, his dick felt like the smallest of the three, that I remember!"

"No, they weren't on the bus. I guess the one had car cause, I heard one of them say something about "your car" and I head a car start after they left the restroom. Coach, ever since that day, I do have to admit, well now to you anyway, that I've always wondered if getting fucked in the ass could be fun, if you were not being forced into it, and maybe have some grease or something up in there to make it work better."

"Coach, I know that on that day I did not like what had happened, but as time went on, I really started wondering what it could really be like. What it could be like if done with someone that cared for me. Someone that did not force it when I tried to tell him to stop. Coach, today is the very first time that I have ever been with a guy to have sex with him, well except for that one day and those guys, and I've always wondered if it could be fun. Coach, can we? I want to finally find out if that could have been fun if they had done it differently."

"Yeah Joe we will. We'll do that if that's what you want! But Joe, who in the hell was the guy that told them you have a big dick? Who told those guys that? Do you know who that was?"

"Coach, I really don't know for sure, but Jimmy Zan used to go to our school and that year his family moved over to Collier County someplace, and I think it must have been him. I didn't see any of our guys talking to those guys. Jimmy had been in gym classes with me when the other guys were always saying that I had a big cock, mine got bigger earlier than most of the guys', and I think he must have been the one that told those other guys. Since mine was a little bigger than those guys at that time, they all claimed that it was bigger because I was a gay. I guess that's the reason that I never allowed myself to ever play with another guy — well until today that is, but hell man — when I found out it was you, there was no way in hell I was going to pass up this opportunity. I know I kind of refused at first, but I was still trying to figure me out. I still don't think I should be wanting to do something like this, but I really do. I've kind of always thought those three guys kind of messed up my mind, and I've never really sorted it out yet. Maybe today will help!"

"Hell Coach, back in those high school days when our team wrestled your guys, I always went back to the locker room with wild ideas of being in bed with you. Your guys, I never dreamt about them, but you, hell yes! Now, you, that was a different manner. Hell Coach, you could have done me when I was still a student, and nobody would have ever found out about it! Yeah man! Yeah Coach! I wanted to have sex with you back then too. Coach, I've always wanted to have sex with you, but because of that messed up day I had, I always made sure I never thought about playing with a guy. You know Coach, I've always wondered if I was, for some weird reason, attracted to you since you are a big muscular black man, and I have to admit that when that black guy was the one fucking me, I think maybe I was really kind of liking it. He hurt, but looking back, I do kind of think I liked him being in me and fucking me. He was a hot looking guy. Yeah, he was young, but hell so was I back then. I was wanting him to do me different, more gentle, because I guess I must have really wanted to get fucked by him, but of course I didn't tell him or the other guys that. I have to admit I've wondered, over the years, just where he is now. Does that say, that maybe, I'd like to do that all over again with him?"

"Shit man — if I had only known over the last few years, or at least since I got out of school, that I could have come to you — wow — shit — how things would have been different! Coach, are you going to try and get that big railroad car of yours up in my ass?"

"Yeah, Joe I sure am!" Then Coach asked. "Joe, how much time have you got available today?"

Joe replied, "I've got as much time as I need. Today is my day off, so I don't have to be home by any specific time, why?"

"OK Joe, here's the why. I don't feel comfortable doing this here at the house. Let's do remember I am a married guy. Not that I expect her, but for some funny reason she could come home totally unexpected, or maybe somebody else could come to the house for some reason. I've got someplace that I'd like for us to go to that I think would be safer."

"Oh OK! Where is the other place?" Joe asked.

"Well Joe, I guess I don't really need to remind you that what I am about to tell you must remain a complete secret, but I and four other married guys secretly rent a small apartment that we can all use when we need a hiding spot. It's downtown in an old apartment complex. I'd like for us to go there. Besides, I've got plenty of Crisco there!"

"Wow! Oh, OK! Hey — yeah I like this idea. Yeah, I like that idea better too. Should I take Troup home and have you pick me up, or you want me to meet you there or what?"

Coach and Joe decided that it would work best if they met at the apartment building in one hour. Coach gave Joe the apartment address and made sure he knew exactly how to find the location. Joe dressed, grabbed Coach's cock and then re-grabbed it with both hands and said, "See, I knew I could get my hands around it, I just have to use both of them at the same time. Shit man! I hope to hell I know what in the hell I am asking for. When I have to use two hands to get all the way around it, then I wonder if asking for it to be put up in my ass isn't a little crazy. Shit man — you will be really very careful with my little ass won't you?"

"Yeah, Joe my man! I will be careful! You hit the road man, and I will see you there in one hour from now! OK?"

"Yeah Coach, yeah! I will be there, scared like hell I'm sure, but I will be there. Oh hey! Is there anything that I should bring?"

"No Joe, everything we will need is already there! Everything is ready! Just bring your ass. That's the one thing that we will definitely need! See you in an hour!"

Chapter Three: I Really Need That Ass of Yours!

Joe found the apartment and Coach was already there, waiting for him.

"Hey come on in man!" Coach said to Joe as he saw him approach the front door and opened it for him. Since the coach was already fully naked and supporting a raging hard-on, he stood behind the door as he opened it and greeted Joe in.

"Oh shit man!" Joe exclaimed as he took a good long look at the coach's naked structure, and his extra long and thick dick. "Shit man! It's only been about an hour since I last saw you completely naked and looking so good, but to see you like that again is a big hard-on, turn-on for me again. Coach, you are so damn hot looking! God man! You are hot!"

"Well, thanks Joe, but so are you! I've admired that body of yours since I first saw you on the wrestling mat your Freshman year in high school. You don't know how many times I had to either get to my coach's office or get home, so that I could jerk off just making believe that you were in the room with me. Joe, I've shot more cum, when just thinking about how I'd love to play with you someday, than all of the cum I've shot when actually with other guys, and trying to act like they were the dream of my life! And when you asked me if I would try to fuck your ass, shit man, it's a wonder I did not just fucking pass out! Get those clothes off! Let me at you! Joe, I gotta tell you man — it is shocking as hell, that you wanna see if you can get fucked with this dick this morning! I gotta admit, it is one hell of a lot thicker than even most of the other black dicks that I've ever seen, and for you to ask for it up your ass, the very first time you are playing around, that is shocking man, shocking!"

Joe started removing his shirt and warm-up pants when Coach told him to leave the tight, form fitting, underwear on for a few minutes. "Joe, those shorts look so damn hot on you, I want to play with you some before you take them off. I want to feel you up. I want to chew and lick on you. I want to feel your ass and chew on your crotch. I am so damn glad you found these in the store the other day and had them on today. I've seen this type of underwear in ads before, and I thought they looked hot on the models, but shit man, on you, and here in person, they are hotter than hell!"

And with that statement, Coach immediately knelt down on his knees and started licking the tight, form fitting, shorts that Joe had on. He turned Joe around and rammed his face up into Joe's ass as far as he could push it! As he bit the fabric and some of Joe's ass skin, Joe moaned a very pleasant moan of approval. He pushed his ass back toward the coach's mouth. He lowly said, "Bite me, bite my butt! Bite my butt, please!" And he then let out another very inviting moan.

Coach chewed and bit on Joe's butt, He bit the left cheek first, then leaned over and lovingly bit the right cheek. He then turned Joe back around so that he could get to the very pronounced crotch. As he looked at it, he told Joe, "Oh man! The way these shorts are made, so that your whole basket stands out so far, and of course with the amount of meat that you've got tucked in there, God man, there is no way a guy's crotch can look any hotter."

The coach then immediately dropped his jaw open as far as possible and forcefully rammed it onto Joe's, shorts covered crotch, as far as he could. He pushed his face in toward Joe's mid-section so forcefully and strongly that Joe had to reach back and grab the edge of a chair to stabilize himself and not fall over backwards. As soon as he steadied himself, he roughly threw his body forward as if to attempt to put his entire body into the coach's mouth. He grabbed the coach's head and pulled it toward himself. "Eat me Coach, eat me Coach! Eat my dick!" Joe, forcefully instructed.

As Coach chewed on all parts of the large protruding and exciting crotch that was right in front of his face, he slipped his fingers into the top waist band of the shorts and started to pull them down. As he slowly pulled on them, the waist band slowly snagged on Joe's raging, strong, hard-on and came to a stop. Coach tugged harder and pulled the waist band down past the big white cock. It flipped out from behind the fabric. The bag of balls fell forcefully toward the floor. The coach exclaimed, "Oh shit man! Shit man I can not get over just how big of a cock you have got for a white guy. Joe, I know some white guys have big dicks, but I sure know I have never been with one of them, or played with one of them, until today. God that is beautiful!"

And with that statement of excitement, the coach immediately threw, actually threw, his head onto Joe's straight rod. He pulled Joe up to him as close as he could, and he immediately took all of Joe's cock down his throat. He pushed Joe back so that his rod would almost come completely out of his mouth, and then he would pull him forward again so that all of the cock would ram itself back down to the depths of his throat. The coach continued this pushing him out, and then pulling him back in for twenty or thirty thrusts. He took Joe's dick as completely as he possibly could each time, and each time attempted to take more dick — dick that was not even there!

The coach then suddenly told Joe, "Come on Joe, let's get in the bedroom. I need to get started on you!"

Coach helped Joe step out of his shorts and get his shoes off and they then went into the bedroom — with the coach's hand firmly gripping Joe's ass.

"Lay down Joe. It's time we see just how much of my dick you can take!"

Joe looked at the coach and said, "Coach, I know I am the one that asked for this, but shit man, I've got to admit that when I look at that damn big dick, it gets me scared to hell, all over again. You will take it easy on me and if I can't take it, you'll stop. Right?"

"Yeah Joe. You are safe. Man, I've put this dick up smaller butts than yours before and they wanted me back in there again later, so yeah, you are OK. I'll listen to you, and if you really can't take it, then we will stop. Lay there, I'm going to finger some Crisco up into your ass, so relax man, right now it is just my fingers."

Joe put some Crisco on his fingers and slowly rubbed some Crisco on Joe's butt, smoothed it around and then slowly put one finger up in Joe's ass. As he slowly and gently rubbed his hand around Joe's ass he then put a second finger up inside. With more gentle pressure, in and around Joe's asshole, Coach then proceeded to put another finger in. Again, more gentle caring with his ass — Coach again placed an additional finger up inside and gently smoothed the Crisco all around.

"I've got four fingers up in there right now Joe. How is your ass feeling?"

"Coach, it's feeling good. You've got four fingers up in me, is that what you said?"

"Yeah, that's right man! I've got four fingers playing around up in there. And that's feeling pretty good. Right? Four fingers is not causing any problem back there uh?"

"No — it's feeling pretty good Coach! You sure you've got four up in me. I really didn't think I could take four fingers quit that easily. They really are feeling good."

"Good man! Good!" Coach replied. "OK Joe, I'm going to take my fingers out and start using my dick. And — hey man, with the way you were enjoying my fingers, I'm sure you are going to be quite OK with my dick."

Coach took his fingers out of Joe's ass and repositioned himself so that he could get his long rod in position to start it's tunnel entry.

"Lay still and just relax man. I'm about ready to fuck your cute, little, marshmallow cream white ass, with my big, long, thick, stiff, chocolate, cock! We are finally going to do it, and once you get it up in you, you are going to beg me to keep it up in there!"

Joe kind of laughed and then told Coach. "Yeah man. Yeah! Right now I've just got to see if I can even get it up in me or not. Coach, take it slow back there man, slow! I know one thing, you call that cock of yours a big, long, thick, stiff, chocolate, cock, and all I can say right now is, I kinda do wish it was chocolate, cause then maybe I'd be able to reshape it enough to get it to go up in my ass without tearing it all apart! I think you are a lot more convinced that I can take that damn big thing much more than I am. Coach, I want it, but we've got to go slow, please!"

"We will Joe. We will!"

Coach got the tip of his mammoth rod positioned right at the opening of Joe's ass. He very slowly started to lower himself down and into Joe's ass.

"Oh shit man!" Joe almost screamed. "OOOOh- wait a minute Coach! Wait a minute!"

The tip of the coach's rod had entered Joe's ass.

"Oh shit man! Oh shit, I thought I was ready for that! Shit man! Is the end of that damn thing bigger than all four fingers you had up in me a few minutes ago? My God Coach! Shit man! That damn thing is so big! Coach! Shit, I'm not sure I am going to be able to take that up in my butt! Coach, that just might be too much for me!"

"No Joe, it's not too much for you. Your ass was just clamped shut since you mentally knew I was going to start putting my cock up in there, and you just need to relax it some. I'll just lay here for a minute or two and let your asshole get used to it before we do anything else."

126

Coach kept his dick from going in any farther. He quit pushing on it and he grabbed Joe by the chest and gave him a hug. The two men, now acting as a one person, with one man in the ass end of the other, laid there for a few minutes until the coach heard Joe lowly say, "Coach, it quit hurting now. Have you still got your cock up in me?"

"Yeah Joe, yeah. It's still in there. See I told you that all we needed to do was give your little cute asshole a minute to relax on it. Feels pretty good now doesn't it?"

"Well yeah, it feels better, but Coach, if it hurt that much when you just put the end of it in, what is it going to feel like if you push it up in me farther? Coach, is it going to hurt again?"

"No Joe! Believe it or not, it's not going to hurt! It's just that first little getting the tip of it in you and getting your asshole to open up far enough for it. That's the only time it will hurt. From now on, it will just feel kind of like you have a real ass full, but Joe, it will feel good! OK?"

"OK Coach. If you say so. All I can do is trust you. At least right now it sure don't hurt me any like it did that day those three guys did me in the restroom. I know your dick is a hell of a lot bigger than any of theirs were, and it doesn't hurt like they did, so I guess I'm still game for seeing how much of you I can take!"

"Joe, the reason it doesn't hurt like it did that day is, we have some grease up in you so that it's not pulling on the insides of your ass. My dick is slipping around in there. And Joe, it will feel better the farther up in you I push it."

Coach firmly grabbed ahold of Joe's chest and slowly restarted his decent into Joe's ass chamber. He slowly pushed down, and very carefully listened for any negative comments or rejections from Joe. He heard none. He pushed further! He heard nothing that indicated that Joe was not accepting his cock with pleasure.

The coach did hear, "Oh Coach! Oh coach — oh man, this is starting to feel good! Yeah, Coach, this is feeling a whole lot different than it did that day I got it from those three! Shit, I wish those guys would have used some grease on me that day. It might have felt good when all three of them fucked me if they had greased me up some. Shit man, I wish they had used some grease on me. I've always wondered what this could feel like, and Coach, today it is feeling good. Coach, how much of your dick have you got up in me right now?"

The coach moved his body slightly so he could look down toward his dick and replied, "Well — Joe. From what I can see, it kind of looks like

127

I've got about half of it up in you right now. I've only got probably about five inches of it up in there so far. You still wanting more?"

"Yeah, yeah, but Coach take it slow. I'm still not sure how much of that thing I can take up in me. I want it, I really do, but shit man, it is so damn big!"

The coach rubbed the back of Joe's head and told him, "I'll go nice and slow. I'll take care of your little butt in a good way. I want the whole dick up in there, so I will go nice and slow so that it just keeps getting hungrier and hungrier! You little white ass is feeling so good around it, it just needs to go in as deep as it can!"

Coach slowly pushed his body against Joe's and allowed more and more of his enormous dick to slide on up into Joe's ass. As he continued to invade the depths of Joe's innards, he rubbed Joe's head and kissed the back of his neck and shoulders. Each time he gave Joe a small loving kiss, he could hear Joe moan with a very pleasant accepting moan. This encouraged Coach to continue not only his deep ass travel, but the other loving movements of rubbing and kissing also. The coach was finally loving the feel and the penetration into the young man that he had dreamt of playing with, and fucking, for so long.

"Oh Joe! Oh Joe I can't believe I finally have my dick up inside of you and your ass! You don't know how long I have just made believe that I was doing this. You have no idea how many guys' asses I was fucking when, in my mind, I was in your ass. Joe I have wanted this little ass of yours for way too long!"

As the coach made that statement, he delivered into Joe's ass the entire length of his dick. He pushed strongly and solidly to reach the very bottom of Joe's ass chamber and as he did, Joe let out a slight moan and with a low volume, a deep grunt and an "Huhhh", but no indication that he was not enjoying it, nor that he wanted it to stop!

Coach asked, "You OK man? You OK?"

Joe reassured his big muscular fucker that he was OK and then added the question, "Are you all the way in Coach? Have I taken that whole thing? Is that whole, big, fat, cock up in me now, Coach?"

"Yeah Joe! Yeah man, you have all of me up inside of you now. You've got it all! See, I told you that you could take the whole thing! Feels good up in there doesn't it? Like it man? Tell me you like having my cock up in your ass! Let me know you like having me up in there!"

"Oh yes Coach! Yes, I do like it! Yes, yes, I do! It feels good up in me. Oh Coach I never thought getting a dick up in your ass could feel good like this. Oh, after that time with those three guys and what I went through that day, I never thought I'd ever want some guy's dick up in me, but oh Coach — I am so glad now that I actually got the nerve up today to let you know that I wanted to see if I could get it in me or not! Oh Coach, yes your dick does feel good to me! Move it around up in there so I can feel it up inside of me! Push on my ass. Push on me!"

With that input, Coach started really enjoying the tight little ass, that he had his enormous, oversized, cock stuck up in. He had finally started his much looked forward to fucking, of Joe's ass. His movement started in earnest and with vigor. He took advantage of Joe's request to get fucked, and now he was actually getting the fist real opportunity to enjoy this sweet white ass.

As he humped and bumped Joe's ass, the coach asked, "Joe, how you doing, guy? You enjoying having my big long railroad car, as you referred to it, up in your ass? You like having the ole coach up in your butt? Wishing now that you had told me when you were just in high school that you wanted me to fuck your butt? Wishing you had been getting this for the last six or seven years? I sure as hell know I wish I had been getting it! Push your ass up in the air. Let me push down in there as far as I can go!"

"Fuck me Coach. Fuck my ass!" Joe had completely lost his fear of getting the big rod shoved up in his ass. He was completely enjoying all of it up in him as far as he could get it. "Fuck me Coach, fuck me hard please! Please, fuck me, fuccccck me!"

"You asked for it man! Remember you asked for it! Here I go! I'm going to fuck your tight little ass as hard as I've ever fucked any guy's ass before!"

Suddenly the entire bed started shaking! Coach was ramming Joe's ass with more force than he had ever used on any guy before. Finally getting to Joe's butt and getting in it all of the way was very, very exciting to the coach.

"Hang on Joe, this bull is fucking you for all you are worth. Grab ahold of that bed. Hang on!"

The coach fucked and fucked his Joe as hard as he possibly could. Joe never made any attempt to get him to stop. After totally exhausting himself and draining sweat from all parts of his body, Coach finally collapsed on top of Joe and pushed his cock in as far as he could push it!

"Joe, I'm going to fill your ass! Joe, I'm cumin! Joe—get ready to get an ass full of cum. Joe—I'm cummmmmin! I'm cummmmmmin man!! Ohhhhhh — man! Oh man, you just got a butt full of black coach cum! I just fucked the hell out of you and then I loaded you and your ass full! Joe, you have got one hot ass man! Shit man, I am going to need that ass often. Joe you have one sweet ass!"

"Oh shit man! Oh shit!" Joe loudly exclaimed as he felt his ass getting filled with cum. "Oh shit man! Oh shit Coach I can feel that in me. Man your cum is warm! Oh Coach I feel like I am going to shoot it out of my ass it feels so full! Oh Coach, I've got my ass full of you and your cum! Oh Coach I like that! Never, never, did I ever imagine that getting it up in the ass like that, could feel that fucking good!"

"Lay still man!" Coach told Joe. Coach rolled off of Joe and for a few minutes just laid there and regrouped. He caught his breath and finally said, "I love your butt and I love fucking it like that. For God sakes Joe, I thought you would tell me to stop or to at least slow down, once I got to really fucking you good and hard, but shit man! I guess you must really like getting it good and rough back there, don't you? You just let me fuck the hell out of you and you never said anything, so I just kept going. Shit man, I was really trying to get you to tell me to stop, but hell man, you love to get your ass fucked! I fucked you rougher than any other guy I've ever fucked before! And, Joe, I thought I had fucked some guys pretty rough before, but man, never like that! I am exhausted! I am fucking exhausted!"

Coach laid there and took deep breaths.

Joe raised his hand and placed it on the coach's chest, and said, "Shit man! Damn, I think I just got fucked! Coach, did I just get fucked?"

Laughing, Coach replied. "Hell yes man! Hell yes — you did get fucked! You got fucked and fucked and fucked! Man, I will need a week to recover before I can fuck you like that again!"

And laughing also, Joe said. "Oh OK! Just wanted to be sure that is what getting fucked is! Just wanted to be sure I had not just imagined it! Shit man, that made my ass feel so damn good. OK Coach, now I know for sure that it can be fun getting fucked in the ass. You convinced me now that it can be fun. You know, I may need that done to me again sometime."

"Sometime?" Coach quickly, and laughingly asked. "Sometime? You had better want it soon and often. Real soon and real often! Joe, if you and I can get together real often, then I'm done with picking up other guys that I have no interest in. Man, if you will let me fuck you every other day or so, you and I can become steady fuck buddies! Yeah — hey — I like that idea! Every other day or so, or even — every day is better!" Coach laughed. "You and me as steady fuck buddies! Joe, tell me we can do that, please! Oh Joe, let me know that I can get at you soon and often — please! I really need that ass of yours!"

Chapter Four: Do Guys Really Do That?

"Yeah Coach, I'm sure you are going to be able to get to this ass just as often as you want. All of a sudden you've turned this little white guy, into one horny cock loving, ass hungry guy. Now, instead of me letting you get at my little asshole anymore, right now, I want to learn how to take as much of that big long black cock down my throat as far as I can, so let's go get in the shower and let me wash my ass juices off of it, so you can give me a little lesson of — take big daddy's big, black, long, stiff, thick, cock into the little white boy's tinny, little, mouth!"

After reaching over and roughly rubbing Joe's head after his last comment, the two men got up from the bed and went into the bathroom. Coach adjusted the water temperature and then reached out, took ahold of Joe's hand and said, "Come here little white boy — as you described yourself. This big ole black man with the big, black, long, stiff, thick, cock is going to get it washed up so that you can use your — as you called it — little white boy's tinny, little, mouth on it and make it feel all good and excited. Let me tell you something! The way your ass takes this big black cock sure proves that you are no little white boy. With an ass that can take this dick as quickly and as forcefully as your ass took it, sure proves that you are one hunky white man.

Don't ever refer to yourself as a little white boy again. You are my big hunky white, ass hungry man!"

Both men laughed and Joe stepped into the shower and started getting himself all good and wet. Coach handed Joe the bar of soap and said, "My back could use a good soaping if you don't mind."

Joe took the soap, and very slowly, deliberately and caressingly lathered up the coach's back, the back of his neck, and under each ear, the arm pit under each arm, down the inside and the outside of each arm, down the sides of the coach's rib cage, and then slowly and very lovingly, slid the bar of soap down between the cheeks of the coach's ass. As he did so, he knelt down onto the floor so that his face was right at the height of the Coach's ass. He very slowly rubbed the soap into the crease of his butt. He slowly and gently massaged and moved each cheek to the side as far as possible and slid the soap bar up. He rubbed the soap to create a nice and thick lather on the coach's butt. He admired the contrast in color of the white soap suds, compared to the dark and deep mahogany skin color.

Using the back of his hand, Joe removed some soap coverage from the coach's left butt cheek, and very gently and lovingly kissed it. He took some of the coach's ass skin into his mouth and sucked on it. The coach moaned a very pleasant expression. Joe then did the same to his right ass cheek, and also gave it some kind and loving feelings. Again, Coach let him know how he appreciated the acts of kindness and caring on his butt.

Joe moved his hands down the massive, strong, solid, leg muscles, and calmly reached around to the front and took ahold of the coach's stiff and raging cock. He rubbed the cock and handled the bag of balls. He squeezed and manipulated the bag and it's contents. He turned the coach around so that he was now face to cock, and with his face placed so closely, he admired the enormous large black rod, the overly large bag, and the oversized balls that were inside of it!

Joe exclaimed, "Oh my God you have big balls! I had not felt them yet! Oh Coach, no wonder you shoot so much cum! My God your balls are the size of big eggs!"

He rinsed the soap off of the coach's bag, and he placed one ball in his mouth. He tired to take the second ball and simply could not get that much into his mouth. He chewed the one ball around in his mouth for a few seconds and then let it fall out, so that he could now concentrate on the big black cock rod, that was brushing up against his face.

After kissing the tip end of it, Joe slowly started to place his mouth on the large head of the cock — he leaned forward, and took a deep breath as he started his first venture down and onto the cock, hanging from the massive, strong, and big muscular coach, that he had actually dreamed of having sex with for years. Dreams that he had never imagined could possibly, ever, come true. Dreams that had, and were now, actually coming to life, and he now had his mouth down, and going onto that dream cock! And, a true cock that was actually larger in real life, than what he had managed to dream of!

As he positioned his mouth onto the massive stick of meat as far as he could, Joe thought, "Oh, how I have dreamed of getting to do this, to this very man! I never thought I'd ever get to do it. How many years I have wanted to do this, to this man, and to this dick! Oh why didn't I let him know years ago that I thought he was hot and I wanted to play with his body, and with his dick! Oh, how I have wanted to see this dick! I never dreamed that I'd get to stick it in my mouth. I've been fucked by him, he has had this up in my butt, and he has shot his wad up in my ass! I've got his cum still up inside of me. Now I've got his dick sticking in my mouth! I can not believe what is happening to me today! Oh God! Oh God, thank you for letting me have him. Oh thank you God!"

Joe continued to force as much of his mouth onto the coach's cock as he possibly could. He kept pulling the coach closer and closer to himself, hoping that he would be able to swallow more and more of that enormous stick if he could just pull hard enough. The stick of meat muscle was just too big for Joe to be able to take more than about one half of it into his mouth! He realized that if he was going to be able to take anymore, then he needed a larger, much larger, mouth and a deeper throat.

Joe pulled off of the cock, and immediately rested his face up against the coach's crotch.

"Oh Coach! Oh Coach!" Joe attempted to say as he attempted to regain his breath. "Oh Coach you have one beautiful cock. You have so much I can't take very much of it! Oh Coach, how can I take more of it? I want all of it! I want it down my throat! Coach, I want to eat all of your dick!"

"Hey Joe, my man! Don't worry about being able to take all of it down your throat. Eat just as much of it as you can. You can take all of it up your butt man, and that is what I think is important. You can take my dick up in your ass and you like that, right? You like getting fucked in the ass with my cock don't you Joe?"

"Oh God yes!" Joe answered with excitement! "Oh God yes I do coach!"

"Good Joe! Good! I want you to be glad you can get it up in your ass and you like it up in there. That is what is important! I want you to like that, because that is what I want us to do as often as possible. Joe, will I be able to do your ass as often as we can get together? Joe, please tell me that you will let me fuck your cute little white ass a lot. Like a whole lot!"

Still kneeling on the floor, looking up at the coach, Joe told him, "Yeah Coach, yeah! I know pretty damn well right now that you will be able to get to my ass just about as often as you want it! I've wondered for years now just what it could really feel like, to get a good fucking up in the ass by some guy that cares about me and about my ass, and Coach, you sure as the hell have shown me, it can be, and it is, great! I just wish I could swallow all of your dick too though!"

"Oh yeah, Coach, my ass feels good! Taking something that damn big up in your ass really shouldn't feel that good — should it? I mean, our asses are not really supposed to be getting stuff stuck up in them, well — OK — so maybe a little dick, but shit man! One the size of yours? Yeah — the one that I just took up my ass? Hell man! I still can't believe that I took all of that up in my butt! Shit man! I am damn glad I did not chicken out and tell you that I couldn't try it, and I will admit, that when I laid down and realized that you were aiming that thing at my asshole, I was really damned scared! Coach, I was! I really was! Coach, I wondered right then if I was really out of my mind for agreeing to do this. I was really wondering if maybe you were just using me and going after my ass since you couldn't get anybody else to let you fuck them. Coach, I guess I was a hell of a lot more hungry to get a guy to fuck me than I realized, or I really don't think I would have agreed to it, and especially after I saw how damn big it was! Coach, I've never even seen some gay porno film where I had actually seen where a guy gets something like that rammed up in his ass. You know Coach, if you had been some weird guy that never gets any ass and you were really setting me up, I could have been left with a torn up asshole. You know, now that I have been fucked, and now that I do know doing it was not dangerous, I'm really feeling kind of real stupid for agreeing to do that without really knowing for sure that I would not get torn up! I guess I really was a hell of a lot more hungry and ready to get fucked by some guy than I realized, wasn't I?"

"Hey Joe! You know damn well I would never do anything to you that is dangerous! You're my man! I'd never do anything to you that would be bad. Joe you have heard of guys that get fisted, haven't you? Shit man! Getting some guy's fist rammed up in your ass, sure is a hell of a lot more than getting my dick up in an ass, so I can assure you that my dick is not going to tear any guy's ass open."

"Coach, yeah, I've heard of that, but do guys really do that? I always thought that was just make believe or funny talking. Coach, do guys really do that? Do they really take some other guy's hand up in their ass?"

"Sure they do Joe. A lot of guys do that."

"Have you ever done that Coach?"

"No, I personally have not. Now Tim, one of the other guys that uses this apartment, is really into it, but I've never done it with him. I've thought about it a few times, but have just never done it."

"So is he the one that gets a fist put up in his ass or is he the one that puts his hand up in some other guy?"

"He does both, Joe. He is a fisting top and a bottom. I've talked to him about it quite a few times, but I've just never done it with him. He wants me to take his fist, and then after I do that a few times, become his fister and fist his ass. Like I said, I've never done it before, but he keeps asking me to, and I figure some day, I'll probably decided to try it, if he asks when I'm in the right mood."

"Coach, I always thought that was just funny talk. Would you think I am kind of weird if I was honest and told you that I'd like to watch some guy do that to another guy? Is that being too weird?"

"No Joe, that's not being too weird. Tim is a great guy. If you ever saw him on the street or somewhere else, there is no way in thunder that you would ever imagine that he gets excited about getting his fist up in some guy's ass, or getting some guy's fist up in his ass. There's different stuff for different guys. That does not make you weird to do that stuff!"

"This Tim, guy. Does he do that very often? Does he do that here?"

"Yeah, he uses the apartment a lot for it, but how often I'm not sure. The only times that I am aware of, are the times that I just happened to be here when he and some other guy is here, and they are doing it. How often he goes to some other place and plays that way, I have no idea. Are you maybe wanting to be here sometime to watch?"

"You don't think I'm being too weird if I told you that, yeah, I'd like to watch that happen some time? I always thought that was just weird talking, and until now, I really never knew that it actually happens, and yeah — Coach — yeah, I'd like to see it done."

"OK Joe, I'll talk to Tim and see what we can get set up. I know he has at least one buddy that likes to do it with an audience, and have people watch him get it in the ass, so I'll see if maybe he, and his Sammy, can set something up for us. I mean, it's OK if I'm here with you to watch, right?"

"Yeah, yeah, Coach! Yeah, of course I want you there too. I wouldn't have the guts to watch it if you weren't here with me. Yeah, I'd need you here. Coach, I really don't understand, how does some guy get started getting some other guy's fist up in his ass? Doesn't that hurt like hell? I mean, yeah I know you haven't done it, but since you've been around Tim and his guys, have you ever seen some guy get it for the first time?"

"No, I've never seen some guy take a fist for his first time, but I know some of the guys that Tim has had here when I was here were not very experienced guys. They knew what was happening, but I could tell that they had not done it too often. They were pretty jittery about it, but they wanted to do it. Nobody ever told Tim that he could not go through with it. I know a few of them have really had to take their time, though. It took them time to get their asses open, so that Tim could slide his hand up in there."

"Well when he does, I mean put his hand up in their ass, does he make a fist? Does he push a folded fist up in their ass? Shit man, that sounds like it would really hurt!"

"No Joe. You don't make a fist. It's just called fisting. You kind of fold your hand up as narrow as possible and then push it in. Of course, since I've never had it done to me, well — yet, anyway, I've been told that once you are up inside, then you can make a fist. Maybe that is why they call it fisting. I know I have watched Tim on a couple of guys, and his arm action, once he is up in them, he acts like he is ramming or fisting their ass as if he does have his hand fisted up. I'll tell you one thing — of the guys that I have seen get it — they sure do like it! I've never seen one of them that ever acted like he was wishing that he hadn't done it!"

"Coach — a minute ago you kind of said something like you had not done it — yet. Does that mean that you are going to? Are you wanting to do it?"

"Joe, my man! I will be very honest with you right now and tell you that until this conversation, I was never real excited about getting it done to my ass, but Joe, if you are interested in it, and you think that maybe it is something that you might like to learn more about, and maybe try, then so am I! I've never had the chance to kind of buddy up with somebody that I really like, and to learn some new stuff along with him, but Joe, if you are willing to learn how to fist and get fisted, then I'd like for us to do it as a team. Man! Just the thought right now, of maybe getting to stick my hand up in your butt, or even more exciting, the idea of you sticking your hand up in my ass is really, and I do mean really, getting me all excited! Joe, this is something that I had never even thought about as a possibility, but shit man — what an excitement! Hey

— earlier this morning while in the back yard, I was just praying that I'd get to suck on your dick! Now I've gotten to fuck you, you sucked on me, and now we are talking about learning how to get fisted together. Joe — I hope you are not kidding. This is really getting me all turned on!"

"No Coach! I'm not kidding. Yeah—I have to admit that earlier this morning I was kind of real stand-offish once I kind of found out what was happening. I still had bad memories of when those three guys did me in that restroom. But I kind of slowly started to admit to myself that this is what I have secretly been praying for, to have happen, some way, and once it got started, I really got all excited about it. You know, as I think back about it, I've known for weeks now that something kind of different was happening at your house whenever I walked by. And though I didn't realize it at the time, now I know I was really praying inside that it was something like this. I know now that whatever was happening, I was hoping that it was something sexual, and with a hot guy. When I started seeing your body through the front window, I guess I was getting more and more excited about wanting to see what would happen next. Coach, I bought those sexy briefs in hopes that I'd get a chance to kind of show off in front of some guy, didn't I? I did that without really knowing what I was doing or why, didn't I? I guess I was really hoping something kind of like this was happening. And since it is happening, thank God it is with you! I guess maybe one of the reasons that I have never let something like this happen before, was because I was afraid it would be with the wrong guy. You know, I still remember those three guys that did me, and I guess I was afraid it would be another bad day like that one. Now that it's you and me, it's not bad, and anyway, I've always wished that I could just walk up to the front of you and grab ahold of your crotch! You don't know how many times I've looked at you and your crotch, while at one of the wrestling matches. I just wanted to find myself alone with you in a dark hallway somewhere. I wanted to feel you up so badly! I wanted to see what your crotch felt like. I just knew you had a big dick! I wanted to see what it felt like! When one of your guys, from your team, was on the mat, I'd sit there and stare at your crotch and just imagine what was inside of those shorts that you wore. I knew I couldn't, even if we did happen to be in some dark place, but I sure did want to feel you! I wanted to know what a really big dick felt like! I didn't know it was this damn big though!"

"Now, I'm finally letting my wishes come out. I'm finally admitting to myself of what I have been wanting to do for a long time. I admit it now, yeah — I have been wanting to do you, or have you do me for a long time. I just couldn't admit it to even myself! Yeah Coach, I want to learn how to fist you! Yeah — I want to put my hand up in your ass! I want to feel the inside of you! I want to see what it feels like to feel your insides. And I want you to feel my hand up in there."

"For some guy, that until this morning, had never even been sucked on before, I sure am starting to admit what crazy things I'd like to do, ain't I? All of a sudden I have now been fucked up the ass with what is probably the biggest cock in the state, I've had my ass completely filled with your warm cum, I tried to get all of your dick down in my throat, and now I'm letting you know that I want to learn how to fist your ass and get fisted back by you! Oh Coach! I've been wanting something like this to happen to me for a long, long time! I've had dreams about you and I doing something like this, but I didn't even know you played with guys. I've been wanting to do this for years, but I just could not face it and admit it. Now I am really, really, ready!"

Chapter Five: I May be Crazy as Hell!

Coach came into the apartment and found Tim getting everything ready for the upcoming events of the evening. "Hey, looks like you've been here awhile." Coach said as he noticed all of the preparations that Tim had arranged.

"No, not too long really. I keep everything pretty handy so that I can grab it when necessary. So Coach, tell me about this new playmate of yours. You two haven't tried the fist thing yet, I assume. Right?"

"No, we sure haven't. We've only had about three sessions together so far, and Joe told me the first day we got together about how he thought he'd kind of like to see it done, and I told him that maybe you and Sammy would be willing to let us watch, and maybe give us some pointers on the what's and the how's of fisting. I'm glad we finally figured out a night when all four of us could make it. You know I've been putting you off in teaching me and letting me do it, but now that Joe and I are playing around and he has expressed an interest, well — I kind of guess that has perked my interest too. I don't know if either one of us will be trying it tonight, but at least we will have seen a guy get fisted up in his ass, and not feel so dumb and stupid about what goes on."

"Hey Coach. You guys don't need to do it if you don't want to, but if either one of you do decide to try it for the first time tonight, you just let

Sammy and I know. Got to admit, Sammy is a pretty good one to get your first fisting from. He is on the smaller side, as you have seen, and his hands are a lot easier to take up the ole asshole than my larger hands. So if you guys want to try it, just let us know."

Just as Tim was telling Coach to ask if he got interested in doing it, Sammy showed up at the door. He came in, all excited that he was going to be doing some fisting and having an audience while he either did some fisting, or while he got some fisting done to him.

"Hey guys, I've go to admit that it really turns me on when somebody is watching while I get a fist up in my ass or put my fist up in another guy's ass. Actually I do kind of think I get more excited when it is a fist going up inside of me. I don't know why, but I must be an exhibitionist when getting fisted. I guess in my mind I know it is like really weird for another guy to put his fist up in my ass, but then I like showing others that I can do that. I think it goes back to my childhood days when everybody said I was no good at sports and stuff. I have always kind of felt that letting a guy do that to me and also letting others watch it happen, was kind of like making up for my less than happy and accomplished younger days. I'd like to get fisted in front of all of my old childhood people and ask them how many of them could do this!"

Coach and Tim agreed with Sammy that perhaps his childhood days were the reasons that he got all excited about getting it up in the ass like that. Coach added, "Yeah, I've been told, and I do believe, that the reason some guys like to get paddled so much is a reflection on their childhood days. I've been told that as a child they were paddled, and now they find excitement in it as an adult. I'll tell you one thing! About six months ago I was with a guy at his house that really, and I do mean really, got all excited about getting his ass paddled as red hot as he could get someone to give it to him. I paddled him for a solid hour and I was actually afraid to paddle him anymore, even though he was still begging for it. Shit man, his ass was glowing red! Not kind of, but I do mean real red! And for him being a black man, that is not an easy task!"

Joe opened the door and came in just as the other three were finishing up the conversation about Coach's friend getting a red hot ass paddling.

"Hey Joe!" Coach said as he went toward Joe and gave him a hug and a kiss. "Joe, this is Tim, and this is Sammy!"

As Joe extended his hand out to shake hands, he expressed his pleasure in meeting both of them.

Looking around the room, Joe then said, "Well, I kind of think maybe things are going to happen in here tonight, aren't they? Being the only guy standing here with clothes on is making me feel a little weird, but I don't think it is the clothing as much as the big can of grease and all of the other stuff laid out. Shit man, this almost looks like an operating room. Just a little more weird."

Joe started to remove his clothes, and as he did Coach gave him a big hug and told him he was glad they were going to watch Tim and Sammy go to it.

"Joe, Tim has been begging me to get involved in this stuff for months now, and I've always put him off, but now that it's you and I, I'm all turned on to learning as much as I can. Tim told me that if either one of us wants to try, either doing some fisting or getting some fisting, to let him know. He did point out that since Sammy has some smaller hands, he is a good one to get a first time fist from. He told me that Sammy's smaller hands slide up and in easier than his bigger hands do. So anyway, if you decide that you want to do more than just watch, you let me know. I know right now I'm starting to get the idea that I just might ask for some action before this whole thing is over. Ever since you told me the other night that you want us to get with Tim and Sammy and watch them do each other, I've been getting more and more excited about doing it too. Now Joe, if I do decide that I want to try it, and you don't feel comfortable trying it just yet, that's OK. If you'd rather watch, I'll have Tim or Sammy do me. OK?"

"Yeah Coach, yeah. I got to admit that right now I'm still feeling kind of like the little neighborhood boy that is going to be peaking through the fence and watching something that I am not supposed to see. Maybe I will relax a little more once things get going, but I got to admit that right now I'm feeling pretty stiff about thinking about having somebody put their hand up in my ass or even me putting my hand up in their ass. I want to see what happens, but I sure can't promise how involved I'll get."

"Hey that's OK, man. Nobody is going to make you do anything that you do not want."

As Joe and Coach were talking, Tim and Sammy had hit the bed, and quickly decided that Sammy would be the fister, and Tim would be the fistee.

"Tim likes to be on his back while he gets fisted." Sammy explained. "Some guys, like me for example, like to be belly down while I get fisted, and as long as it feels good to the guy getting it, it really doesn't matter. I mean after all, it's all to just feel good getting it, so use whatever position you prefer."

Sammy positioned the big beach towel up under Tim's ass and lower back and rather jokingly told the two observers to always be as neat as possible, so that when the fun is over, there is as little clean up to take care of as possible.

"Hey men, when you pull your fist out of some guys' ass, you'd rather lay there and hug him, and not have to start doing the old washing everything down before you can relax. That is the reason I use the Latex gloves. When you smear this much grease on your hand, it is a whole lot easier to just rip off the glove and throw it in the waste basket than to try and quickly wash this much grease off of your hand. Now hey, guys! Some bottoms do not want you using gloves when they are getting fisted, so always find out first if you should or not. You sure don't want to piss off some guy that you are just about to slide your hand up into. Don't make for too much fun that way."

Sammy had gotten his hand and Tim's butt hole all greased up and then slid some fingers in and out of Tim's ass to kind of get it all excited and ready for an entry.

As he got Tim all ready, Sammy explained the whats and the whys of what he was doing, and the best techniques to use to get his hand up in Tim's ass as quickly as possible.

"After all men." Sammy said. "When you've got a hunk like this on the bed, his legs up in the air, his ass all greased up and starting to get hot, you will find out that you get pretty excited yourself, and you get pretty anxious to be feeling the inside of his ass. Once you do this a few times, the rush of getting in there and feeling around will hit you."

Sammy folded his hand, pointed his fingers and slowly started to enter Tim's ass. He watched Tim's face, and he watched his ass, making sure that everything was OK both with Tim, and with Tim's ass. Tim let out a little groan.

"Hey men. That is what you want to hear. You don't want your man just laying there all stone quiet and silent. You want him to groan some, so that you know he can feel you invading his most private hole, and you also know he is feeling good about what he is feeling up in there."

"Oh shit man!" Joe exclaimed. "Coach, look! Sammy has almost all of his hand up in Tim's ass already! Tim, don't that hurt?" Joe asked.

"No not really." Tim replied. "I'm not going to be a complete fool and try to tell you that for the first few times that it does not hurt, but after you get it a few times, your ass gets used to taking it, and your mind can only think about the joy you feel of having some guy's hand up in there. Really guys, once you get used to having it some, you want it as often as you can get it! Fucking in the ass is good, but fisting in the ass is pure top quality sex!"

Coach and Joe bent over to get somewhat closer to the action, and both men gasped in surprise as Sammy pushed his hand on up in, far enough that his entire wrist disappeared up in Tim's ass.

"Oh my God!" Joe almost yelled. "Oh my God Sammy, how far up in him are you going to go? Oh God, that has got to hurt! Tim, doesn't that hurt? He has more than his whole hand up in your ass!"

"No Joe, it really feels good to me! He's gone up in me, up to his elbow before, and I'm hoping he can do that again tonight so you two can watch it. Really guys, I know it looks like it has to be really painful to me, but it's not. It's a real turn on to me just knowing that he's going up in me like that!"

With Coach and Joe sitting on the edge of the bed, the leaning on each other and watching what was happening between Sammy and Tim, was getting Joe all hot and bothered.

"Hey man!" Coach said as he noticed that Joe was supporting a major hard-on. "It looks like this is getting you kind of all turned on man! You have a raging hard-on!"

Joe looked down at his own cock and said, "Yeah, I guess I do, don't I? Shit man, I was so damned interested in seeing what in the hell was happening up here with these two guys, I didn't even know I had gotten hard. Yeah, I guess this is make me horny, and maybe just like you! Coach, look at the boner you are showing!"

"Yeah, I know! The only thing is, I knew I was supporting a woody. I felt mine go real hard right when I saw Sammy push his hand up in Tim's ass and let his wrist disappear up in there. That really got me all hot an bothered, and I knew it when it happened."

Coach reached over to Joe as he spoke and rubbed his cock. Joe returned the favor. Both men sat there stroking the other guy, and at the same time watched what was happening between Sammy and Tim's ass. As for Tim, they already knew that he was simply laying there in a complete glory taking all of the action in his ass with a complete joy!

"Yeah Sammy, push man!" Tim said as he rather raised up to see how much arm was now up in his ass. "Come on man! I want to show these two guys what it looks like for a man's arm to disappear up inside of another guy. Push it up in me. I want to feel your hand up inside of my chest area. Come on man! Fist me real deep!"

"I'm trying man!" Sammy replied. "Lay still there and give me some more time. I'm working my way up in you as fast as I can. When I get to my elbow, I'll make sure you know it so you can look down and see it. I know from the last time we did this, that your seeing my arm that far up inside of you, is a real turn on to you, isn't it?"

"Yeah Sammy, yeah! Yeah man, I like it, but I don't get it often enough. We have got to get Coach and Joe broken in so they can be fisting me too when you are not here. Hey man, I'd give up fucking all together if I could just get fisted about every day instead. I love it man! It feels so damn good to me! Put your arm up in me!"

"Oh God Coach, this is getting me all turned on! Coach, I did not expect anything like this to happen. Hey, Coach, I don't know if I can take it or not, but the way I feel right now, please play with my ass. Coach, finger my ass. Oh Coach, this has gotten me all hot and bothered. Shit man, I'm going to be honest — I'd love to feel your hand up in me. OK! Now I've said it! I'm sure I will regret it if you even start to try, but that is the way I'm feeling right now, so I decided that I had to just day it. Coach, if you play with my ass and I change my mind, you will stop won't you? I know I should not have said that, but my ass is getting real anxious to be played with, so if you will promise to stop if I ask you to, I'll let you do some shit to my ass. Play with it! It's hungry for some hand action back there."

Sammy asked Coach if he wanted to use a glove, or go bare handed, and Joe rather interrupted and told them that he really doubted that Coach was going to be going in far enough to need a glove, but Sammy told Coach that he ought to use one anyway, since he would be smearing some grease all over Joe's ass anyway.

Coach put on a glove, asked Joe if he wanted to lay on his stomach or on his back, and after Joe decided that he wanted to be on his back so that he could see, Coach started smearing some grease on Joe's ass.

"Oh God yes!" Joe exclaimed with pleasure as he felt Coach's hand hit his asshole. "Oh yeah man, put a finger in my ass. Please Coach, finger my ass!"

For about the next 15 or 20 minutes Coach played with Joe's asshole and slowly but carefully started to open it one finger at a time. During this same time, Sammy continued to work on Tim's ass and continued to make additional headway in getting his arm up into Tim's body interior.

"There Tim, I'm in to my elbow! Can you sit up a little and see it? See, I knew it was not a fluke the last time that we did that! You've got a lot hungrier asshole than what you think."

"Oh God that's hot!" Coach said. "Shit man, that is fucking hot! Joe can you see Tim's ass? Can you see how fucking far Sammy is up inside of Tim?"

"Yeah I can see it, and it is making me want your hand up in me that much more. Coach, I know damn well that I can not take that much up in me, but I want to get your hand up in me if we can. Can we try? Coach, I want to know that I got your hand up in my butt tonight. Oh God I'm crazy for saying that aren't I? Oh shit man, I know I am going to be fucking sorry that I ever said that!"

"OK Coach. It kind of sounds to me like you have a man there that is ready to try and see if he can get fisted. You willing?"

"Yeah, I'm willing, but I'm just not too sure of what I'm supposed to do."

"Hey all you do is keep slowly pushing on his asshole, and watch his face so you will know if he is feeling good or if he is having some pain, and just try to put as much hand up in him as you can. Just push on that ass nice and slow!"

Coach took Sammy's instructions to heart, and slowly attempted to put his hand up inside of Joe's ass. Joe jumped a few times, but each time, he told Coach that he was sorry because he did not want Coach to quit, but for just a moment or two it had hurt. Coach turned his hand a few times and actually found the best position to be in that he knew was the most comfortable for Joe. Often Joe would let out a, "Yeah man, yeah, —that feels good, push!"

When Coach heard those instructions, he followed his command, and he did actually gain some success. He could feel that he was opening Joe's asshole completely.

"Joe, you OK?' Coach asked.

"Yeah man, yeah! I'm OK. I can feel your hand and I know it is really spreading my asshole, but Coach, I may be weird, but feeling that hand up in me is really turning me on. You OK? Can we keep this up a little longer? Can we see if I can really get it up in me?"

"Yeah Joe. Yeah we can keep it up! I'm having my fun down here too. I never thought that the day would ever come that I would be trying to put my hand up in that hot ass of yours, so we can stay at this until we do what we want. You just tell me if you have to stop, OK?"

"Yeah I will, but not yet! I like feeling your hand. It hurts the way my asshole is getting all spread open like that, but I guess I'm a weird guy. I like feeling it hurt like that! Oh Coach, I always wondered what it would be like to have some guy do this to you after I heard that guys do get fisted, but like I told you, I thought it was all just talk. Oh Coach, thank God you got me into having gay sex. Oh Coach this is great!"

As Sammy continued to feel the insides of Tim, and also let Tim enjoy the feel of having a man's hand, his wrist and his lower arm completely up inside of himself, he watched the progress being made on the bed beside himself.

"Coach, I've got to tell you, you've got one hot hungry guy there. You've almost got your whole hand up in him, don't you?"

"Yeah Sammy I do. It feels like I'm almost completely in. It feels like I've just got my knuckles to go. All of my fingers are up in there."

"OK man." Sammy replied. "You almost have him fisted. All you need to do now is push one more time, and let those knuckles pop in. Joe, I am going to be honest with you and tell you that when Coach pushes on you enough to let those knuckles pop in, it is going to hurt. It will only hurt for a few seconds, but I don't want to lie to you and tell you that it won't. Coach, when you pop in, do not pull your hand back out! Push it in, and keep it in there. Joe is going to have the natural reaction of trying to pull away from you when he feels your hand go in, but you have got to keep your hand up in him. If you pull back out right away, it will hurt Joe twice as much. Stay in him and let his ass relax on your wrist. OK? Understand? Joe, you hear what I said? I know that when his hand pops into your ass you are going to have the natural reaction of trying to get off of it. Try to relax on it. As soon as the pain goes away, you are going to have the greatest feeling up inside of you that you have ever had. Go for it guys, just take care of each other."

Coach looked at Joe and smiled. Joe looked back at Coach and smiled but then said, "I must be crazy as hell. I know damn well from what Sammy has told me, that this is going to hurt, but Coach, I want to know I had your hand up in me tonight, and so I am willing to take the pain just to be able to say I did it! Whenever you are ready, just tell me that you are coming in. I promise to try not to pull off. Oh God Coach, I really do want to feel your hand up in there. Fist me! Put your hand up in my ass!"

"Joe, I'm coming in!" Coach suddenly said as Joe told him to put his hand up in his ass. Joe screamed in pain, and he jerked and did try to pull his ass off of Coach's hand. Coach remembered what Sammy had told him, and he forced himself to continue to push against Joe's ass, although he too felt like he needed to pull out.

Suddenly Joe relaxed. He took a deep breath and said, "Oh God man! Oh God! I've got your hand up in me, don't I? Oh shit man, I've got your hand up in my ass! Oh Coach, I like that! Yeah, it did hurt for a second, but that quit. Oh Coach, wiggle your fingers. I can feel your fingers up in my ass. Oh God Coach, this is hot man, this is hot!"

Coach looked at Joe and grinned. He then looked at Sammy and Tim and just said, "We did it! I've got my whole hand up in Joe's ass! We actually did it! I'm actually fisting him! Shit man, just a few days ago he had never been sucked off before, and now he is laying there with my fist up in his ass. My God he was ready for this! This guy was more than ready for getting active with some good gay sex. I've got me a gold mine here men! I've got a gold mine!"

Coach continued to play with Joe's ass, and the inside of Joe's ass, as did Sammy in Tim's ass, although he was in much deeper. Joe had looked over once and told Coach that he wanted to learn how to take it in all the way like Tim had done, but he knew that had to be on another night. After about an additional 15 minutes of true actual fisting, Coach watched Sammy pull his hand out of Tim's ass, and he then followed suit on Joe's ass. Once again Joe felt the pain of having Coach's knuckles pop out of his hole, but the pain passed much more quickly this time, and all Joe could ask for was for Coach to massage his asshole and kind of make love to it. It did not hurt, but he just felt like he wanted it to be loved and for Coach to make sure it was all still together so that it could be used like that again, and soon.

"Oh Coach," Joe said. "Never in my wildest imagination did I ever think that I'd even ask you to put your hand up in my ass tonight, let alone my actually getting it up in me, but now that I know how damn good it feels, I really do want us to try and get me fisted like Tim got fisted tonight. I want it up in me all the way to your elbow — like Sammy did to Tim. I know I may be crazy as hell, but Coach, just as soon as we can, I want to try that! I want your whole arm up in me, as far as it will go! I'm really, really ready for that now!"

About the Author

Wade Wright

Wade Wright is an older gay gentleman, (using <u>his</u> wording here now) that lives in Arizona, alone, except for his puppy of about 15 years, and is semi-retired. One "normal" marriage, and two sadly shortened gay partnerships, have given Wade a perspective of living very different types of lives, and wishing some of his stories were from "true life adventures!"

Wade Wright is also the author of *Apartment 117*, *Yes, Cops Do It,* *—Oh Yeah*, and also *The Two Straight Guys* available from Amazon.com, The NazcaPlainsCorp.com, or your local bookstore.

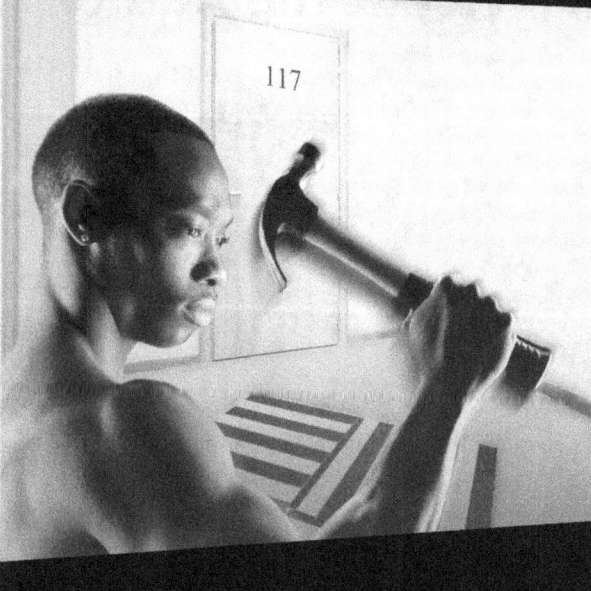

WRIGHT

APARTMENT 117

APARTMENT 117

117

a novel by
WADE WRIGHT

A
BONER
BOOK

Wright

The Two Straight Guys

The Two Straight Guys

a novel by

Wade Wright

A
BONER
BOOK

WRIGHT

"YES, COPS DO IT, — OH YEAH!"

"YES, COPS DO IT, — OH YEAH!"

a collection of stories by

WADE WRIGHT

A HOSER BOOK